The Narrows, Miles Deep

a novella and stories

As Raymond Carver once wrote:
"So much water, so close to home."
This is the deepest.

All best,

Tom

3/2022

Tom Schabarum

The Narrows, Miles Deep

Cover photograph ©2011 by Tom Schabarum
ISBN# 13: 978-1456596637

Contents

The Narrows, Miles Deep

for Jayson

I am haunted by waters.

Norman Mclean

Part One

"There's no accounting storms like the one we had yesterday. They blow in up from Mexico full of rain, dump it all in minutes and then disappear or dwindle down to nothing. But yesterday, now that was something different..."
Bob Blumenthal, Channel Four News

"It took a long time to determine there was anyone missing. The only way we knew those two boys were missing is that they never came back to their camp. I expect they could be down in Lake Powell by now or lodged in some canyon. They'll turn up. People always do."
Deputy Parker, Hurricane Junction - Utah

"How do you bury a son? Very slowly. Especially in Eric's case... and especially when there's nothing to bury."
Monte Morris – Owner, Wasatch Trucking Company

Laura Morris

I'll never believe my boy is gone. Eric was always running at full speed, always hard to catch home. I don't think I've ever called him up and found him on the other end of the line. I hate those answering machines. We've never needed one. Someone's always home. He knew he could always call and someone would be here. I mean, couldn't they just look up and see the storm coming? You can here. You can see storms come from way across the valley, see the far mountains go to black, see the rain raising the dust off the fields. I'd always told him to watch the horizon for trouble. And he could always come home. If I couldn't help him, then maybe the Bishop could help. Bishop Jack always had an answer, and an appropriate reading to refer to in the Book of Mormon.

I don't guess you bring a boy into this world thinking they'd find themselves in some kind of trouble, much less die before his time - before you. It's a hard thing to accept. Monte goes into work earlier now and stays later. There's things he won't say or talk to me about. I keep thinking this'll work itself out, but I'm not so sure anymore. Eric was our only boy. Samantha is off in the East starting up the school year, making noises about coming back home, but I tell her there's nothing here. Salina's turned into a one-note town. There's been talk of capping off some thermo-gas, like they did over in Cove Fort, but they've been talking about that for some time. I don't expect that'll bring in too many jobs. We seem to just be a place for heading off to somewhere else. It's been perfect for Monte's trucking company. He can send trucks up into Denver or Salt Lake easy as you please - or all over the West - you just had to pick your onramp.

When Eric came off his mission he moved to Salt Lake City and began

11

working and going to school up there. He came home from serving the church different. After two years, he was still gentle and sweet, but was unsure of himself where most of the other local boys came back with plans, married old girlfriends, started families. Eric just wanted to get away. I didn't understand, but I suppose the thing to do was just let him be. I wish I had gone slower when I was his age. I didn't want him to miss a thing.

Cargo

It's so hot the wheels slap under the truck. Coming out of Baker, where the world's tallest thermometer reads higher than a hundred and five, Roy is hooked into cruise control, hooked into the music and imagining the weekend ahead. He's been on the road since early morning and wants to make Las Vegas by one to hit Southern Utah by five. In Vegas, he's picking up his old boyfriend and he's thinking to himself how he'd like to rekindle the romance, and wonders if things will be the same. It has been four years since the break-up.

Eric went off, became a trucker for the family business, traveled all over the West. Roy settled into his first job out of college - engineering in a small firm. If he had it to do over again, he'd have joined Eric on the great adventure of the West. Duty won over wanderlust, and the two met to make love one last time in the cab of Eric's truck on a Friday afternoon, before he had a pick-up in Pocatello.

The Blazer has picked up a rattle somewhere under the dash, so Roy slams his fist down hard to make it go away. American cars, he thinks. The truck is only six months old.

Late fall and it's still scorching, the sun hot through the window and into his chest. He's got his shirt off, baseball cap low over his eyes, Bruce Springsteen reverberating through the cab of the truck.

He's got a cargo of camping gear in the back - a tent, stove, sleeping bags, boots. He has white gas stored carefully for there are things that he still treats with care. He has two blow-up mattress pads, because even though he's still barely thirty, he knows what comfort means, and how to achieve it. He also has a camera to record how Eric looks now. How close he is to the memory he has of him: blond, blue eyes, a body that tapers down into a fine shape, a face like a moon - round head, flat features - a voice with a Janis Joplin scratch. He

13

remembers how he felt - smooth and hard across the back and butt, soft over his chest and firm furrows down his torso.

Roy tries to stop thinking about him. What if everything is different? What if there's still that wide gulf between them after they'd split. Has time allowed it to close up? He concentrates on the road, settles in for the rest of the drive, is glad to have a brand new car, his first one, with air-conditioning.

Amanda

"I'm between boyfriends. I can do this." Eric said to me. I was over picking up a sweater my girlfriend, Donna, left behind the other night.

"Are you sure it's a good idea?" I said, and folded the sweater up and tucked it under my arm. I thought Eric ought to get a maid to clean his place once in a while. There are dishes stacked in the sink and on the counter. His bed's unmade, dirty clothes are all over the bedroom floor. It didn't use to be like this, but I've said my mind on his housekeeping skills too many times lately, so I just kept quiet.

"Yeah, it's a good idea. It'll be good to see him. It's been a couple of years anyway."

"Who called who?"

"Does it matter?" Eric had a cooler in the middle of the kitchen. He filled it with stuff from the refrigerator - Cokes, lunchmeat, red licorice vines (Roy's favorite), some apples. "He called me, but the trip was my idea."

"Donna thinks you should go, but I'm not so sure."

"You should be on Donna's side."

"Donna's a sucker for camping. Maybe she should go with you. It'll give me a free weekend." I laughed at this. I was thinking I could've used a free weekend. Do all the things I wanted, but never did because of Donna.

I love to wander the casinos in the summer because it's cool and feels like night all the time; all those jangling machines, coins cascading down into the pockets and buckets of old men and women. But I never gamble. Addiction runs through my bones. I just stare, sidle up to someone who is on a roll and watch the money flow. It's seductive, but I know that if I reach up and pull just one of those arms, there would be no end.

"No, just guys this weekend," Eric said, "besides we're heading up to Lake

15

Mead in a couple of weeks. You're going, right?" He folded a t-shirt to my amazement.

"Do I have to?" I knew I had to. It had become an annual thing that trip to Lake Mead. It was the Fall Jumping Classic. All of us jumped naked into the water below from these impossibly high cliffs, which scared the bejesus out of me, but Donna loved it. She tied her brown curls up in a big floppy mop, then painted all the boy's toenails, painted her own, took red lipstick and drew arrows down the boy's stomachs to their private parts and dazzled me with a seductive cliff-side dance to music she played in her head. Then - and this was just as the sun set - we all jumped out far from the cliffs and into the blue lake and swam to shore where we lay out until we were chilled and then climbed up and drank tequila from the bottle. Donna called it heaven. I went along because it was part of the deal to be in love with her, part of what I needed.

Donna

There was no one that was more fun to go camping with than Eric. He'd pack all kinds of shit to go with us. It was like camping with a portable Ramada Inn. He even had a shower that he'd hang from a tree, fill up with water so that it warmed in the sun all day, and then at night, after a full day of hiking, there'd be hot water to clean off with. He also had this big stove with two burners that he'd set up and, instead of those usual camp dinners, he'd sauté onions in thick butter so that the smell would drift through the campsite, bring stares from other campers who were wrestling with their pathetic little campfire stoves. He cut the vegetables expertly, thinly. Then he'd throw them in with little bits of garlic. The smells would change, people's faces tilted to the air like dogs sniffing the wind. On the other burner he'd boil pasta. At the exact moment that everything was al dente, he'd toss them together. You could hear the slight crackle of the pasta hitting the hot, buttery pan.

I was in charge of the wine, but that was it.

Eric would call me up on a Friday, have me packed and ready to go in four hours, and at some exotic place I never thought to go. We always arrived at night. In the morning at sunrise, he woke everyone up to see the view, which was always spectacular. In the time I'd known him, we'd covered most of the four corners area, the Eastern Sierra and parts of Colorado. Sometimes Amanda went, sometimes not. But she always made the Fall Jumping Classic and he brought whomever he was seeing at the time: skinny guys, a heavy-set one and another who was flawless and smart, but not very nice.

Once he brought Roy - it was the first time I met him - and I could see what the attraction was and thought that they should have worked harder on staying together. They understood each other, almost as if they were both clairvoyant. Even Amanda and I aren't like that. We really have to work hard, but I tell her that we're like geese, that we're mated for life and we're not supposed to break up despite the miles we travel to get to a mutual understanding.

When we arrived that time at Lake Mead for the Classic, I watched them together as they unloaded Eric's truck, worked the tent up and put together the camp. They did everything silently, but together. It made me want to cry at the time because I wanted that so much for Amanda and me. For the rest of the weekend, I couldn't take my eyes off the two of them when they were near each other. It was like they were twins.

Conviction

Roy's on the final descent into the valley where Las Vegas sits at the far edge. Cars can be seen miles down the road and the waves of heat makes it look like there are more than there really are. One of the things that he can always count on is the spectacular view out across the dry lakebed. Only once had he seen it full of water. It had rained nonstop for a month and the water came down off the sides of the barren mountains and filled the basin. Water sloshed over the interstate. Traffic was routed into one lane and backed up for miles.

That was the last time he came to see Eric who'd graduated after the winter quarter from the University of Las Vegas and threw a big party - invited practically everyone he knew - and insisted on him being there.

When he arrived, the party was in full swing. People were bundled up in corners. Men and women sat in each other's laps or draped themselves across each other. There was every configuration: two women, men and women, and a large group of gay men in full color. Collectively they were known among their friends as "The Showgirls." Some of them had come directly from working the early show at the Desert Inn where Eric worked reservations and special group sales. They had kept their costumes on, but had removed the attachments of feathers and sequined crowns that wouldn't fit into their compact cars. Their outfits were tight, what little there was of them, but they enjoyed the shock value they had on people like Roy. He walked nervously between them looking for Eric. He was afraid to ask where he was, afraid to be drawn in and questioned. Most of them had to get back for the midnight show, but while they were there, they made it known that they were indeed, there.

"Hey, handsome." Roy recognized the voice and turned. Eric held out a beer to him. "You need to get started."

"Sorry I'm so late. I couldn't get off work as early as I wanted to." He worked in Los Angeles as an assistant engineer at a construction firm; one of those kinds that slap up houses in planned communities. Lately, there were cutbacks and he didn't feel like he wanted to risk a couple of hours because his boss was in the office, which was rare, and he wanted to keep appearances.

He stepped up to his former lover and took him in his arms, gave him a kiss and held it. All of the feelings he had for him came rushing back, moved through him as water through a canyon. There is love left here, Roy thought as Eric took a step back to look him over.

"You've got a little belly." Eric laughed, "I like it."

"Yeah, I'm corporate now. Three martini lunches, fried hors d' oeuvres every Friday, no sex."

"You need to move." Eric took him by the hand, "Come with me." He led him outside to the balcony. Roy had a hard time finding the apartment which was just one of hundreds in a huge complex that seemed to cover a city block. Their outsides were sand-colored stucco and the same, reminding him of the houses his firm built in the deserts and valleys of Los Angeles. Eric squeezed his hand and let it go. "You look good," he said.

"Just a second ago you said I was fat. Do you think I'm fat?"

"I didn't say that…. I said you have a bit of a belly. Which I said I liked."

"Really?" Roy had gained weight and it bothered him. Working out took a backseat to working and there was no reason to be in shape anyway. He'd stopped dating for a long time, had moved into a self-imposed exile after Eric. Even after two years, he still hadn't the desire to search for someone new. A guy would have to throw himself in front of him, like a person committing suicide by running onto a freeway. They would have to be that forthright in their conviction to break the shell he'd created.

"Yeah, you look great."

"Thanks. Congratulations by the way." Roy hugged him again, hard, too hard. He wanted the feel of him.

"Yeah, finally, eh? Never too old to graduate." There was an awkward moment as the conversation stopped. Roy looked over Eric's shoulder at an oncoming couple of "showgirls."

"Honey, we have to leave so that we can assemble ourselves." One of them reached over and air-kissed him so as not to smudge his make-up. The other came up behind him and pecked him on the ear leaving a bright spot of red on the lobe. Eric laughed.

"Now you keep that there, love," the ear-kisser said. "I want to know that no one else has been there when you show up for work tomorrow."

"I won't even shower." Eric patted him on the butt, sent the one on his way.

The other eyed Roy, who averted his look. Light bounced off the sequins of the man's tight, brilliant red costume, pin-lights swirled over him as if from a mirror ball. It was the smallest topcoat and tails he had ever seen. The man had him mesmerized because he was so foreign to what he was used to.

"You're gorgeous, pooch and all." The man reached over and lightly touched his stomach. He made a mental note to hit the gym and start eating salads when he got home.

"Roy thanks you. As do I." Eric moved up next to him, rubbed his belly like it was a magic lantern.

"Shazam!" Roy shouted. Both the showgirl and Eric jumped. He walked away from them and into the cramped apartment. He didn't look back.

He sat down on the couch in the living room, and fended off questions about where he was from and how he knew Eric, and what he did for work. It had been a long day and he found himself fighting off sleep. He was polite, but his speech began to slur after three beers, his head lolled back against the couch and before long he was out.

Todd

"So what do you think we should do?" Eric had been distant with me most of the night, but I wrapped my arms around him anyway.

"We should wake him up and put him in your bed." He broke away from me because I think he was uncomfortable with my affection in front of Roy. It was after the party and we were cleaning up. He opened all the windows and the sliding glass door to rid the apartment of the smell of beer. We cleared the apartment of bottles, leftover chips and plastic dip cartons. Eric held a garbage bag for me while I tossed everything in. Roy remained asleep, but I could feel Eric stealing glances at him behind my back.

I studied Roy when he arrived and saw that Eric noticed him immediately. I wondered what he felt when he saw him. Roy had a scar above his eyebrow and a nose that bent slightly to the left. He was softer, whiter. It looked as if he'd been locked in some office; the fluorescent light must have made his skin blue rather than the brown/red that Eric had shown me in the pictures from their time together. Did he remember how they were when they made love? I wanted to go up and touch Eric, lay some claim to him, but then I also wanted to see them react to each other. I could tell he still had a longing for him, but Eric had me then, yes, and I was wonderful to him.

A beer bottle rolled across the carpet. Thankfully it was empty, but it missed the lip of the garbage sack, hit my toe and rolled toward the balcony. I said, "Keep the bag open and pay attention."

I went for the kitchen and left him standing there mesmerized by the sight of Roy again after two years. Eric went over to where he was sleeping and kissed him lightly on the forehead and gently shook him. His eyes fluttered open, then rolled back in their sockets. Eric picked him up and carried him down the hallway and into the bedroom as if he were carrying a sleeping child. Alarmed, I followed them.

"What are you doing?" Roy half-consciously awoke and brought his arm around Eric.

"Moving you in here," he said as he hoisted him up onto the high bed and pushed him over so that he would be more in the middle.

He pulled Roy's shoes and socks off, undid his belt and pants and slipped them off. It was almost clinical, I thought, but then I noticed Eric slowing as he took in Roy's legs, the fine hair that ran from his inner thighs down onto his ankles, the lovely shape of his calves. When Eric noticed me at the door, he quickly brought a blanket up over his former lover's torso.

"You still love him," I said.

"I do, but in a remote sort of way." Eric passed me and left the room.

Later, when we were making love, I could tell he wasn't thinking of me, but of Roy. The one thing men are incapable of doing is going through the motions when they make love or they just lose it. So I stopped what I was doing and moved up over him and brought his face into mine to try and bring him back.

David Bancroft

My son, Roy, could always sleep. You can tell a lot about a kid by the way he sleeps. When he was but a tadpole, I just sat and watched him in his crib. You could see him thinking all the time the way his eyes moved and how he brought his tiny hands up and winked them away. People don't understand this fact about babies. They get so wrapped up in the daily work of them, they forget to just sit back and watch; how they entertain themselves, work out problems in their tiny little noggins like they do.

Roy was the quietest little baby you ever saw. Melody, across the street, used to always remark on his silence. She'd drag him up into her arms, look down his mouth and say, "He's got a tongue and voicebox, doesn't he?" Then she'd slap his little behind to get some response, but he only smiled and squirmed his way to the ground.

You couldn't attribute it to the lack of a mother because she hadn't up and left yet. He was as tight to her as butter to bread. When she did leave though, he just got quieter.

Summer evenings I could hear the neighbor kids all the way down the block. They'd carry on past ten o'clock, and old Mr. Hargrave would yell at the top of his wintery lungs for them to shut up. Our house might have well have been the neighborhood library or hospital. People would naturally hush as they walked by. I watched mothers yank their children's arms if they made a peep. Sometimes I wanted to go out with one of those one-man-band contraptions and make some noise. I wanted to shout down the cul-de-sac and let them know that even though we'd seen hard times we were still alive, still here.

My life has been about numbers, most of them diminishing. Roy came out six minutes after his brother, but he was the one who lived. We were four people suddenly, then three, then two. I don't think Julie ever got over losing Roy's twin and every time she looked at Roy she saw the other. I think it drove her a little bit crazy. Well, maybe not a little bit. She did just up and leave. She left without taking anything: not a stitch of clothing, no pictures of her family or ours, or even a bit of food for the journey. She left the car in the driveway like she always did and the keys were still on the hook behind the service porch door.

Roy knew something had changed, but not a sound came out of him and I could never tell whether he missed her or felt she was gone. He sort of took it as fact that she might never come back. I suppose he had a sense that some part of him was missing too, but we made a choice to never tell him about his brother when he was born. We didn't want him to grow up missing something he could never miss. But twins have a sixth sense about things, and I guess his being quiet meant that he was always waiting for something to show up, something that would make him whole, make things good.

Maybe him turning queer was like him reaching out to find his brother.

Pie

Roy woke wondering where he was, how he got undressed and into a bed that didn't feel like any he'd ever been in. Roy had a thing for having just the right bed. He liked high ones that you sort of hop up onto. He liked firm mattresses that felt lived in, and those soft, cottony mattress covers with sewn pillows filled with fluff that made Roy feel, on cold mornings, like burrowing in.

He remembered Eric carrying him from the couch and into the bedroom, then everything else was a blur save for the light touch from Eric down his body and over his underwear as he undressed him.

He got out of bed and went into the kitchen and found orange juice in the refrigerator. It was left over from the party and used to cut the vodka that was partially left in three separate bottles on the counter. Roy pulled a plastic cup from the remaining stack and filled it. The juice was tart, pulpy, store bought. His face soured, but then the taste mellowed and he drank the rest as he stood there in his boxers, looked down to see if they were adjusted right, and then reached to close the flap that stood open exposing himself to the apartment.

The place wasn't really much of an apartment. The outside, cookie-cutter façade matched the inside. Cabinets were made of cheap pine, the carpets were a grade above landlord carpet - the kind that has swirls and bumps to hide years of tracked-in mud - the walls were painted beige over textured drywall. Roy's natural aversion to this kind of housing came from engineering it. His company forced him to strive for the lowest common denominator building the houses they did to keep costs down. To actually find himself standing half-naked in something that approximated the culmination of his work scared him a little. His inclination was to bolt before anyone else was up and head back to Los Angeles.

Instead he looked for coffee, found it and fixed some. He was upset that he'd missed most of the party. He'd wanted to watch Eric among his friends, see what he was like with them. He envied his ability to put everyone at ease. It didn't matter who they were. They just fell under his spell. Much like Roy did when he met him at one of the only two gay bars in Salt Lake City.

It was an off night, a Tuesday. Fall folded into winter, ice crystals formed on the windows of cars overnight, leaves past their color lifted off the sidewalks. Coming from California, Roy wore more than he was used to and more than most of the people he saw who'd grown used to the cold slowly, like animals whose fur thickened with the turning weather.

Roy searched the bar out from a guide he bought before he moved to Salt Lake. Walking in, he noticed the stench of cigarettes, could almost feel it entering his clothes like wet fog. He was on a mission to get laid because it had been three weeks since he left Tim back in Los Angeles.

He moved through the bar as if he were a cat - silent, watchful, with disdain. People hovered in corners, hovered over the pool table, over the bar that extended like a ramp of excess down the long room. When Roy got to the back bar, where the lights revolved and the music thumped through the heart, he saw Eric immediately, dancing, sweating, moving his arms in small circles. He was dancing with another, older man who was oblivious to him and was sloshing a drink around in his hand, maintaining a breath of seriousness about the business of dancing with someone like Eric. The world seemed to stop on its very axis as Roy stood in the back, in the shadow of the doorway, in the black of anonymity while he watched Eric move.

The smoke dissipated some, more from swirling bodies than from the fans lazily turning above. Roy shifted his feet, leaned back against the doorjamb. The song segued into another and then another. The two men kept on dancing, building up heat, making Roy more nervous as he thought of possibilities with this guy. Another man came up and asked Roy to dance and he accepted only to be nearer Eric, maybe smell him, see him up close. He couldn't begin to tell you what this man looked like today.

When they started dancing, Roy maneuvered himself so that he had a discreet, but full view of Eric. He never looked directly at his dance partner, but over his shoulder. Roy would tell you that their eyes met then, but the truth is Eric never looked his way in the two minutes he remained dancing with the older man. He was left to finish out the impossibly long song, whose rhythm never changed and whose insistent beat created a dull ache in his head. When the song was finally over, he excused himself, said thanks over his shoulder, wound his way back to where he'd been standing and gave up.

From behind him a voice said, "You're doing a good job holding up that wall." Roy turned and it was Eric smiling, very white teeth, a bulging vein at his temple ready to explode if necessary - he was fascinated. Working through witty responses and finding none, Roy simply stared at him, found his pockets and thrust his hands in as far as they would go.

"You're mighty handsome." Eric said, laughing, fingers coming up to Roy's shoulder. "Don't be scared."

"I'm not scared."

"Then take your hands out of your pockets and let's see them." Roy pulled them up and held them out.

"See, they're shaking."

"Just a bit cold, I guess."

"You just got through dancing. How could you be cold? I should be cold. I just had to go outside with my friend, Frank, who had to have a cigarette, but hates smoking inside. It's forty degrees out there." Eric took Roy's hands in his and started rubbing them together, but they felt like they were shaking from too much caffeine. There was nothing he could do to get them to stop.

"You were dancing, too," he said.

"I was." Eric let go of his hands, but Roy held them up. "That felt good. Don't stop."

"Your name is what?" Eric asked, "and give me your full name." He brought his hands under his arms.

"What are you doing?" Roy was aroused. He was young. He was broken now and would do anything if only for one night, but he felt it wouldn't be for only one night, so Roy stayed careful with himself.

"Warming you up." He squeezed down on Roy's hands. "It all starts with the hands. Now, your full name?

"Roy Taylor Bancroft."

"That's a good name. It's got a whiff of nobility."

Eric smiled and removed the warmed hands from under his arms. He held them a while longer and then let go. He seemed mildly calm, but unsteady as Roy moved away. He leaned into him. He smelled fresh soap among the cigarettes. He dropped his head to his shoulder and let it rest there.

Roy didn't make a move to pull away, but instead brought his hand up around Eric's head and held it there. It was kind of spooky, this instant attraction. He knew the feel of this man and knew his smell: honey, oak and vanilla. Why did it seem so familiar to him?

"You smell good," Eric said.

"Except for the eau de cigarette, I suspect." They parted and Roy shuffled back a step.

"Yes, but it's got a twist of something, lemon, mint?"

"Menthol." They both laughed and Eric moved toward him again as if he was intent on keeping him near.

"I'd say that we should go outside, but it's too cold. Been there." Eric made a move to guide Roy into the other room where the music wasn't so loud, but where the smoke was heavy and thick. Roy stopped and took stock of the situation, decided something to which Eric responded, "Want some pie?"

Later he would tell Roy that pie always worked for him - Peach, Strawberry, Blackberry - all the summer ones. He'd tried the cream kinds and didn't like those. Fruit pies reminded him of watching his mom work strips of dough over their tops, taking a special fork handed down from her mother, and her mother before that, and crimping the edges while spinning the pie around.

Eric said, "I don't want sex or anything, just pie."

Roy was impressed by his candor and nodded yes.

"I was thinking of the all-night diner at the bottom of the Ramada up the road where pie's their specialty." Eric moved him towards the door.

In the booth, Roy fidgeted with the condiment tray. First the salt, then the utensils gathered in a glass, then he pulled out the napkins one by one. The diner was empty except for a couple with bombed-out stares.

Eric watched him remove the napkins, then reached over, gathered them all up, squeezed them into a roll and deposited them back in the glass with the utensils. "Relax, okay?"

"I can't." Roy slid against the back of his bench. "I don't want to get into all the particulars of family and that stuff. I hate that."

"That's fine. I don't like it either."

"I've got to ask you one thing, though." Roy leaned into the table, rubbed his hand along the edge of the Formica to see how sharp it was. "Are you Mormon?"

"Why do you ask?" Eric shifted in the booth.

"We're in Utah, that's all."

"Not any more." Eric seemed uncomfortable with the question. "I'm working away from it at the moment."

"Just wondering, that's all. We don't have to talk about it."

Eric threw his arm up over the back of the bench to get ready to explain. "It's fairly new, talking about not being Mormon. My whole life was about working towards my mission, saving the money to go, trying to fit in like my friends, realizing that it was a waste of so many years. I've been a Mormon all my life and to not be able to reconcile it with what I am today is hard," he said.

The waitress came with menus, smiled at them and told them the specials. While she spoke, Eric hooked his ankle around Roy's foot, held it there. Roy had been concentrating on the choices of pie, remembering the way she'd said "apple cinnamon" musically, dramatically emphasizing the breaks in the words. He wondered if she was an actress because her voice rang through the empty diner. He also wondered if people could see under the table. It was getting fairly late in the evening, just past eleven, but still, anyone could just walk in and see their legs entwined. Ordinarily, Roy would be more cautious, would probably not be eating pie with anyone. There was a wide gulf between taking a guy home from a bar for sex and sitting down with someone. It wasn't in his make-up to do this, but if this was how the game was played in Salt Lake City, well then, by God, he was going to learn.

It was more than that though, and he could tell they both knew it. Roy liked the feel of Eric's leg against his and the man had known instinctively where it belonged.

Laura Morris

The real truth to my loving Eric starts with baking pies. Since I can remember, he'd stand over me and watch me build them from scratch - first I cleaned the fruit, then peeled and diced, or cut them into wedges if they were peaches or apples (the berries I'd leave whole). Instead of white sugar, I always used the sweeter, denser brown sugar because you can taste the heavy sweetness of it. The flour I kept coarse, put some un-sifted wheat into it so that the fruit juice soaked the crust as the pie baked. I'd put him to work mixing flour and eggs, made him get his fingers dirty because I believe that the harder someone works on something, even if it's just a small contribution, the more one appreciates the end result.

In spring and summer, we made pies on Saturdays for Sunday dinners and the rest of the week. I made five or so and one extra for Bishop Jack who lived alone in a cottage next to the stake house. I always fixed his up last to make it special. I brushed a little egg white on top of the pie to glaze it and add white sugar to make it sparkle. When I started working on Bishop Jack's pie, though, Eric left the kitchen. He'd get out of there faster than I could call after him so he wouldn't have to run the pie over to the bishop's house. I never understood that. Maybe it was him pulling away from the church. The Bishop always liked my pies.

Donna

Eric had these amazing hands. They were big and always warm. He wanted to use them, he said, so we enrolled in massage school together. People winked and nodded when we told them what we were doing. Although, when I said it, it had the ring of truth because I was no beauty and tipped the scale far further than one might expect. But Eric was beautiful, even to Amanda and me. We couldn't keep our hands off him and took him to bed with us when he stayed over sometimes just because we thought that to be near beauty, even if it was a guy, would stave off the inadequacies we felt about our looks. We'd both been virgins with guys when we met each other. I guess that's part of why we brought him into bed with us. He was the closest we'd ever come to having a man against our bodies, though we had no desire, or intention of doing anything other than having him in our bed. It was a way of feeling a man, getting close to what it might have felt like if we'd been attractive enough, or outgoing enough, or popular enough in high school to have actually done it with a guy. We sandwiched him between us and nearly crushed him, and he lay there like a child who had climbed into his parent's bed early in the morning.

I decided on massage school because Eric begged me. I was in need of a job and something to do with my time. He did it because he truly believed all that New Age nonsense about the hand's healing power. It made him really good, and I ended up looking for another line of work after about six months of trying to build a client base. I never asked him how he got so busy so quick, but he assured me it was legitimate and had kept his number out of the back pages of those newspaper handouts you get on street corners in Las Vegas.

Eric ended up getting certified, I didn't. One night I was trying a technique he taught me on Amanda. I had her lying on her stomach, her breasts pushed out from her body like parentheses, containing the largeness of her. I was running my thumb down the side of her spine, working her flesh deep against the bone when she rolled over and told me that if I didn't stop, she'd be injured for life. That about did it for me.

I was okay with it really. Amanda always told me that I didn't have to worry about money. We live up in Henderson in a really nice house, built by Amanda's brother who built homes as a hobby. Neither one of them had to work. But Amanda always worked.

She was the one who dragged Eric home to us one day. She'd been all day at the restaurant her parents started a thousand years ago. They had already made their money, set themselves up for life with investments made all over the city. But Amanda still went in to oversee things almost every day. She walked from table to table to talk to the regulars. Her parents had forbidden any gambling to go on inside the restaurant so that people could relax, get away from all the noise, enjoy some peace and quiet.

I'd make dinner for Amanda and me - always something complicated because I had the time - and we'd sit outside in the fall, winter and spring and indoors, with the air on full blast during summer. We'd gather the dogs, scurry them outside and they draped themselves over our feet while we ate. It was so much domestic bliss it was disgusting, but it was comforting to me after the chaos of my growing up.

When Eric began coming over more frequently, after his break-up with Todd, I'd just started buying groceries in quantity at the Shop n' Go where he'd meet me sometimes to make sure that I was making him his favorite dinners. I suppose that was why he never let me cook on the campouts, giving me a break from it. He knew there were times I needed a break from the duty of living with Amanda.

How do you sustain love - all the work - making it look seamless to the outside world? I suspect Eric knew how hard we worked at staying together and helped us through it, which is why we loved him so much. I knew we both went to him with complaints about each other, but he just listened, offered suggestions and never let on that myself or Amanda had just visited with him hours ago to tell our particular sides. I'm a sucker for love and Amanda is addicted to me.

Home

On the way to his apartment after leaving the diner, while the headlights to Eric's truck flooded his car, Roy began to sweat slightly though the heater hadn't yet kicked in. He rolled the window down and let the cold air dry his forehead. He fiddled with the dials on the dash of his Honda to keep himself from looking back, but he made the turns slowly, signaled every corner, made sure that he and Eric had no chance of getting separated.

They climbed up into the avenues, a section of the city that had views across the valley. From the homes that stair-cased up the hill, you could see snow flurries in pockets tumble down out of the clouds. Storms wedged themselves against the Wasatch Mountains. The valley lights flickered like colored beads, turning the night into something magical for Roy.

He waved at Eric to park on the street and went up the driveway and behind the house to the carport. He'd rented a basement apartment under the home of a young couple. They were graduate students at the University who'd married a year earlier and finally got around to fixing the downstairs into a small single with a large room, kitchen and bathroom. They advertised the apartment as furnished which meant it came with a couch, coffee table and bed that all said hand-me-down. But they installed new carpet, put framed posters of skiers jumping off snow cornices, Rainbow Arch at sunset, a summer meadow. Roy signed the lease agreement for six months knowing that he would move into something larger when the paychecks came.

The couple was nice enough. They had invited Roy for dinner, made him wine-drunk the first night he was there. Roy felt they wouldn't mind once they found out about him. Still, he snuck Eric in like a thief. He turned the light on in the apartment and was embarrassed at the boxes that littered the room, still taped shut, or half-open with their contents spilling out on the floor. It was all he could fit in the Honda, but the smallness of the apartment made it seem there were more than there really was.

Though heat is supposed to rise, the apartment was stuffy and warmed by the furnace that clicked on and off all night behind the bedroom wall. It had kept Roy awake the first night to the point that he began to curse and was thinking of breaking the lease. He wondered if he could get it annulled like a bad marriage. He wondered what Eric was thinking. He hadn't spoken yet and simply stood by the open door letting the cold air in. Roy was all excuses as he went around and swept up his things and tossed them back into their boxes and pushed them into the corners.

Eric came up behind Roy and wrapped himself around him. "I don't care how it looks," he said, "we're not using this part of the room anyway."

Roy relaxed a little, turned. Their mouths met, tentatively at first, then hard.

They made love through the night until Roy heard the creak of hardwood floors overhead. The sheer cotton curtains let in the outside light. Eric stirred and went under the covers and nuzzled Roy between his legs, but he made Eric stop what he was doing and brought his head up next to his so he could whisper as they'd done all night.

"First, Clare gets up, goes to the bathroom. Then a flush, then Paul. I've been here two mornings now and I already know their routine."

Eric moved into Roy, who moaned.

"And what's going to be our routine?" Eric asked as he pushed.

Roy gave into him and closed his eyes. "This," he said.

The night went well.

In bed with Eric, Roy had the feeling of being solid, whole. It had nothing to do with how they made love. The sex was good, but there was an emotion that came in - so little was said - but Eric had revealed himself to Roy through the night by the touch of his hand on the side of his head, his cheek resting on his thigh, the flick of his tongue across the tip of his nose. These were small things to be sure, but the value of them was sustained and made stronger by some unknowable connection.

When Eric went to clean up, Roy came in to watch him and sat silently on the toilet seat, eyes intent on his form. The running water steamed out of the spigot, the smell of soap held in the wet air. The bathroom tiles glistened with sweat.

As Eric cleaned himself, and ran water through his hair, Roy thought it was more exciting than getting into the shower with him. It would have been cheating he felt, like joining in on one of the most private things one does. Glass doors on showers were like windows into another world - the excitement he felt at discovering it was unsurpassed.

After, they went back to bed and began the whole process over again as if it were the first time. It was a sensation that Roy hadn't felt before. When they spoke, Eric said that he'd always been casual about sex, treating it as if it was only a need, a fulfillment of the body. Mormons didn't talk about sex except to repel any feelings they might have. The possibility of love was supposed to only come up once in their lives, at an impossibly young age, and then children were to be made of it.

In the middle of their lovemaking Roy shuddered. Eric kept his head up against his neck. When his body shook again, he pulled him in tighter.

"I'm sorry," Roy said.

"About what?" Eric tried to calm him.

"About this." Roy's crying subsided as he brought his arms up to Eric's shoulders. "I probably shouldn't have done this tonight. I kept mulling it over in my head at the restaurant."

"Do you want me to go?" Eric moved over on his side. The room was changing, getting darker - it was as if a deserted road had lost the moon.

"No, no. I just don't know where it came from, that's all." Roy sat up against the pillows. "Maybe it's being new here and leaving everything behind like I did."

"What do you mean by everything?"

"My family, friends…. I had a lover."

Eric inched away a little. It was just enough to use as a signal that the night could possibly be over.

Roy reached out for him and ran a hand along his shoulder. "The lover wasn't serious. We'd run our course." He searched for words; "this just all seems so new to me. I've done everything we've done before but I feel like we're attached in some strange way. You touched my forehead like my mother used to do."

"Is that okay?"

"It's the best thing you could have done." Roy smiled and made up the distance between them, moved into the pocket of Eric's torso with his back and pulled his arm around him. They moved against each other again and the morning light filtered in, filling up the room.

Roy hadn't thought about his mother for a long time so it surprised him that Eric brought her back to him. He'd held the memory of her in a small box inside himself and let it sit there, wearing itself down, smoothing the edges like stones in water. It helped him to believe that she would have come home someday, would have walked through the front door of his father's house and told them that she'd lost her way for a time, but now was back. But it never happened and Eric endured a succession of his Dad's girlfriends and acquaintances because he could never settle on one woman again.

Roy and Eric finished as the racket upstairs became louder; the shower turning on, a morning news program, toilet flushing, the constant back and forth of footsteps from one room to another. Roy again had the thought that he couldn't endure this every morning for another six months. Maybe he'd get used to it, but he'd never lived under someone, had always lived in a house or on the top floor.

Eric fell asleep again and Roy turned over in his mind the last comment he had made: "What is going to be our routine?" It excited him and made him fill with expectation. He could not remember a night so devoid of awkwardness. Waves of emotion overtook both of them; meaningless words were never said because some gap needed to be filled.

Roy decided to wait until all of the sounds were gone from upstairs and he'd heard their car in the driveway leave before he'd let Eric go. But as he stirred, Eric took a look at his watch on the makeshift nightstand of boxes. It was a Wednesday and Roy didn't start his job until next week, but Eric had to be up and to work in an hour. The night was perfunctorily over. Eric collected his clothes and dressed. Roy searched for his sweats, not wanting to say anything about waiting for his landlords to leave, and sat on the edge of the bed putting on socks. Now the awkwardness came as they finished dressing. Neither one brought up the exchange of numbers or made the effort towards a pen and paper. There began the dance of a successful one-night-stand; both wondered if it was going to turn into two nights. So they stood behind the front door and looked at each other, and then the moment passed and Roy opened the door. He followed Eric out to the edge of the sidewalk. The air was very cold as he stood and held himself while Eric started his truck, waved and drove off. When he turned, he saw Claire standing at the front window, smiling and mouthing "Good Morning" which made an opaque circle of fog on the glass.

David Bancroft

My luck to be single again at thirty-seven when Roy was eight. The number of women I'd dated exponentially grew as I got older and I became less interested in wanting to spend time with just one woman. I tried to shield Roy a bit from the sheer volume of them. I didn't want him getting the wrong idea, but I think he finally figured out what I was doing; which was going home with them and then getting up to leave before I fell asleep. Sometimes, I slipped up and was crushed when I came in the back door to find him alone in the kitchen sitting at the table waiting. At first I'd lie - tell him I'd been out to pick up something at the store, but he'd say "I tried coming into your bedroom but it looked like you hadn't been there." When he was eleven, I just sat him down and had a heart-to-heart and told him what was up. He never fussed about it, but I went on a long trip of guilt just the same and curtailed my activities for a bit.

I tried to do all those things you're supposed to do with your son. We played catch, went to baseball games, football in the fall, enrolled him in the scouting program some of our neighbors were in. He just didn't seem that interested in any of it. So we gradually stopped going and he left his Webelos group one day and never went back. I didn't try to ask why, I just sort redirected him a bit: I took him to the beach, up to the mountains, got him a dog. When he turned sixteen, he'd load up big, sloppy Trevor in the back of his mini-truck I'd gotten him and be gone from Friday afternoon 'til late Sunday.

Another father might not have allowed his son to do that at sixteen. He'd probably question the motives of the kid, wonder if he was doing alcohol or drugs, taking a girl with him, but I knew Roy wasn't. It concerned me that he'd take off like that, but I knew he'd be okay, though we had an understanding that he'd call if there was trouble.

Los Angeles is a tough place to bring a kid up. So many outside influences and you're not around anything but concrete and strip malls, car fumes and dirty gutters, and kids from all kinds of backgrounds, and constant news of beatings and violence. How does a kid shield himself from all this? Let alone a parent?

Roy just had this natural wall against bad things. He never let them bother him - or at least not that I saw.

What a wonder it was to see him come home from his weekends and pull his camping gear out of the back of the car and spread it over the lawn to hose it all down. Dirt came streaming off the bottom of his tent, his backpack he'd empty out of wrappers and tin cans, dirty clothes. Trevor would be off to the side waiting to get under the water himself, sometimes sneaking in from behind for an early start on his bath. I'd go out and help Roy hold him. There would be that moment that I'd feel like his father and then it'd pass like an apparition, leaving me cold, shaken and longing to start my life over again.

Faith

Roy went back to bed after Eric left. He tried to sleep, was tired to be sure, but filled with so much energy that he got dressed, grabbed his daypack and left his little apartment. He went to the mouth of Big Cottonwood canyon and stopped at the 7-11 there and loaded his daypack with snacks and water. There was a dusting of snow on the peaks, the leaves on the aspens and dogwoods were as bright as new coins flashing, the air was cold and thin.

His gutless wonder of a car began climbing the hill in pain (reminding Roy to get it tuned for altitude). Roy could almost hear it saying "I think I can, I think I can." He coaxed it up through the narrow canyons and over the bridges by talking to it and watching the engine gauge for signs of explosion. It didn't matter that a line of cars began forming behind him, he just hunkered down and wished hard that the car would make it and knew that on the way down his little Honda would redeem itself.

He reached a turnout and pulled over. A stream of cars passed him, some honked, some drivers, he was sure, held the finger up in disgust. He looked over a long meadow, the stream and the gold trees that started beyond it and went up the sides of the mountains. He got out of the car. The air had lost its warmth, but the sun that came was bright and warm against his black sweatshirt. He looked down the mountain road which had now emptied and saw all the way out to the valley from where he'd come and across to the Uintas, another range of mountains that completed the geography of the Salt Lake Valley, that and the large lake looming across the horizon. He pulled his daypack from the backseat and slipped it over his shoulders, locked the car and scrambled down the short embankment.

As he walked he thought of his dog, Trevor, whom he'd left with his dad. He'd gotten old and stiff over time and couldn't move very well. Roy thought that the cold here would make it worse, would probably be the end of him before long and his Dad had agreed to care for him until he died. He thought of getting another lab, but he needed to get settled and see what was what. Plus, the awesome responsibility of caring for a dog held him back. Still, on days like today, he'd love to see Trevor bounding over the low shrubs and in and out of the water.

When he reached the stream, he began following it up the canyon, stepping lightly over rocks, which he was good at, and avoided the loose stones by knowing their look, the way they held against the rushing water.

He was surprised at his energy. He'd slept a total of one hour the entire night and yet he felt he could hike for hours. It was a giddy sort of energy and every so often he had to stop and slow himself down or he'd miss something - a creature, a formation of rock, the way the clouds shadowed the mountains around him.

He spent an hour walking the main river, then followed a smaller stream which cut up into a narrower canyon. The edges of it seemed darker, wet. The sun skipped this particular canyon as if it had lost its trajectory. The air became sweeter - damp wood and moss, oxygenated fern. Roy added a layer of clothes, took out a chocolate bar and ate it. Then he drank some water and was pleased at the taste of it, or the fact that he couldn't taste it like the water in Los Angeles.

Far from the road and the cars, Roy could only hear the water, a slight rustling of leaves, a bird overhead. How many times had he gone off like this? Hundreds? Thousands? The solitude of it had kept him straight up, had given him something of value, transported him over the hump of loneliness. Never knowing how to act in a group Roy always felt awkward and insecure. He'd work the edges of them, picking out someone who he could talk one-on-one with, but he had a hard time hearing in crowds so he'd lean down close, watch the other person's lips, and smile when appropriate.

Reaching an outcropping of rock, he swung his pack up and dragged himself after it and turned to look out over the larger canyon. There was every color imaginable: reds, yellows, ambers, golds, greens. His eyes mixed them together to create new colors.

Roy liked this time of year the best. Things slowed for him and settled as if the earth were absorbing him with the falling leaves then taking a moment to restore itself before winter, and before spring awakened with its changes.

Eric's touch came back to him. Like his mother's: lightly on the forehead. He began to think of her, to equate her smell with the smells of the canyon.

He'd lost the specifics of her years ago so that now she came to him unfocused. The weight of her shape lingered in his mind, however, and he could remember her warmth when she bent over him before he went to sleep, or came up behind him to see what he was doing at the table. It was her warmth that wouldn't leave him. Years went by and no matter what he did it still clung to him until last night, when it was replaced by Eric's. He felt a kind of freedom now, a lightness. He brought his hands together as if in prayer. He smiled, and then wept.

Daniel

I ran into Eric on the street up in Salt Lake one day about four years after our Mission together. I ended up not liking him very much and was glad when it was over. It was strange seeing him again. He was very quiet that day. He told me he'd left work early and was working at some trucking firm, ordering parts through computers, I think. He looked tired anyway.

We'd been selected to go to Caracas, Venezuela because of our facility with languages. We spent eighteen months there before they pulled us out, but not before we'd been offered everything under the sun; girls, drugs, tobacco. We bicycled all over town and down to the beach. Small boys came up to us, offered their sisters or mothers, pulled syringes with amber liquid ready to go, marijuana and bright pills from their pockets. At night we'd go home and Eric would lay on his bed and weep, homesick for Salina where he knew everything. He asked me how a church that he believed in since he was very young could thrust him into a world such as this.

At the Mission Training Center, they put us through crash courses in being a missionary. They gave aptitude tests, linguistics exams, passages from the Book of Mormon to be memorized, clothing guidelines and assigned us as companions for the remainder of the mission. When Eric met me, I could tell that he thought there was some compatibility test missing when they paired us up.

The church believes that two missionaries together kept the other from straying. Missionaries are required to spend every waking moment with each other. Eric began playing cat and mouse with me, an awkward kid from Minnesota. I had dark hair, blue eyes, was black Irish and my family had converted a generation before from Catholicism to Mormonism because they weren't that far off from each other. The holy men they pay homage to were much the same in that they revered their Pope, and Mormons their Prophet, and were selected in much the same way, by a hierarchy of Apostles that had come up through the church as wise old men.

Towards the end of our training, before we all went out into the world we were taken to the Mormon Temple for a ritual to accept the "endowments" of the church. We were given our temple garments to wear underneath our clothes, reminding us of the oaths we took to serve the church and that we were now "endowed with power from on high."

Barred from any communication, we stood in the temple room, nearly naked and accepted our garments, which had the mason's symbol on one breast, a triangle on the other and a compass sewn into the cotton fabric. We slipped them on and now were required to wear them every waking moment save for sports or showering. They took some getting used to because they were more like a one-piece 20's style bathing suit than real underwear.

That night, back in our room at the Training Center, Eric saw me in them and laughed.

"What's so funny?" I asked, adjusting my garments because they kept hiking up so as to make me look like Humpty Dumpty.

Nothing," Eric said, continuing to laugh.

"They don't fit right."

"No, they sure don't. You should make some adjustments to them."

"Really?" I turned around. "Where?"

"I don't know. Maybe make it into two-pieces."

"You can't do that."

"Why not?"

"What if someone saw?" I pushed and pulled at the fabric.

"Who's going to know?" Eric got up and started to adjust the garment.

"When they do the laundry."

Pointing to my belly, he said, "You could cut it here, all the way around."

I said, "I wrote my mother to make some larger ones for me."

Eric went into the bathroom, stood and looked at himself in the mirror, at how ridiculous he looked. He shouted back to me, "I look like Pa Kettle."

"Who?" I asked.

"Pa Kettle from those black and white movies."

"Pa Kettle was skinnier."

"Just the same. I look stupid." Eric came back in the room, shut out the light and went to bed.

On the mission, Eric gradually began to change, though he tried to keep it hidden from the Elders, the Mission President and me. He led me down the alleyways of Caracas, our bikes clattering over the rough roads. We saw laundry hanging from lines strung window to window, diapered infants standing in a patch of sunlight with baby blue walls angling up from mud-caked sidewalks, women sitting on stoops pulling at their hair. We smelled the stench of poverty: open sewer drains, standing pools of water infested with larvae from all kinds of insects, rotting food waste. Boys selling their wares seemed to prey upon us. Eric became reckless and dangerous because of what we saw. He started talking about the hypocrisy of the church selling itself for no other reason than to increase its tithing which he had learned had grown into billions of dollars a year. He complained that the money wasn't being put back to where they took it from, but rather saw the building of the new Stake house, a new temple in Caracas, another mission center, everything to feed the church, not the people.

I wanted to express my concerns to the Elders, but he kept me off-balance during the remainder of our tour of duty. I began hating him, but I never said anything, which was how I was brought up and how we did things in Minnesota. By not talking to Eric, I tried to make his time in Caracas that much more unbearable. But Eric didn't care - not about the people we were supposed to convert, not about me, and especially not about the church.

"How could a church demand ten percent of nothing, which is what most of these people in Venezuela had?" He'd say after a home visit.

But some of them were rich and here he would lay it on thick, suckering them in and then going for the kill just for sport. All I could do was sit back and watch.

One night, we were sitting in a large white-washed living room on the outskirts of Caracas. Eric had his Book of Mormon open, a finger resting on a passage. He pretended to quote from it, but generally made it up as he went along.

"So here it says that all people can reach the kingdom of heaven through brotherhood, through a deep sense of belonging to something bigger than themselves." He'd go on. "Mormon's believe in the strength of families and by looking at your family, I can see that you believe that too." Eric did his benevolent best and raised his eyes to meet the family in front of him

Mr. and Mrs. Ortega nodded their heads, as did their young children who were dressed in a material like velvet - a dress for the girl, a suit coat for the boy - four people for him to save.

Again, he'd go on. "But I can tell that your family is searching for more of a community. I could tell that on the way here, seeing how you live among the other people of Caracas. You are shamed a bit by your wealth?" There was no response from the Ortega's so he took another tack. "You are worried that your children will not learn how to live in God?" Again, blank stares so he went for the jugular, "You anticipate that when you die there will be no one to accept you into the kingdom of heaven. Wouldn't you agree?" He looked over to me, smiled. I was was bewildered, but was a believer and four more people added to the church was better than none. We both looked across to the family.

A tentative nod from Mrs. Ortega and then Mr. Ortega, then the children sat dumbly by their sides wondering what was said. Eric's Portuguese had been sufficient when he got there, but by the eighth month it was nearly flawless.

We left with signed documents, gave them a brand new Book of Mormon. I followed Eric out the door. He started to laugh and couldn't stop.

Eric's eyes had opened.

The Church is uncompromising in its teachings about homosexuality and how it starts with the abuse of your own flesh. But, in the morning, when Eric woke, he masturbated, not caring if I saw or not.

I caught him making furtive glances at a good-looking kid from New Mexico who had a certain amount of Mexican blood in him to make him go even darker under the hot, Venezuelan sun. They sat across from dinner one night at the mission center where they were staying for a few days until another home or apartment could be found for this kid and his companion. They were being transferred to a smaller city inland. We shared quarters in the rear of the mission center. To take a break from Eric, I took the time to get away from him and get to know Antonio's companion.

Eric and Antonio stole away that night. Only Eric returned.

In the morning there was a search party for Antonio who hadn't come back to the mission center. In an hour, he was found hunkering and crying in some bougainvillea bushes down the street. He'd torn his temple garments away from himself and they were lying on the ground. The mission President coaxed him out slowly and wrapped a blanket around his scratched body. Eric stood off to the side and avoided eye contact with the naked boy. Antonio never said anything about what happened, so shamed was he, but he was shipped home the next day for breaking the rules of missionary life - for leaving his companion unattended for one, and for two, leaving the confines of where they lived during off hours. Antonio learned that Mormonism wasn't like Catholicism; you were never forgiven.

I looked at Eric standing in front of me, the Mormon Temple looming over him like a dark cloud. Why didn't I ever say anything to the Elders about him? I guess I didn't want to be a victim of guilt by association. I'm married now - one kid, a good job, a good standing in the church. It seems so long ago, but I do remember one thing. I remember being afraid of him.

Laura Morris

We all drove up from Salina to Salt Lake City to bring Eric home from his mission. We were a caravan of four cars, and other friends joined us at the gate where he was to arrive. Samantha, his sister, bought him balloons and made up a sign with some friends at the high school. She and Eric's Aunt Judy held it high over their heads. Monte was fidgeting with the camera. I guess I was oblivious to everyone coming up and touching me, patting me on the back. I'd put all my energy on that door that leads to the plane. You could see it there getting attached to the arm of the walkway. Snow was coming down hard at the time. The whole outside of the airport and all the other planes and such had disappeared. Some friends had offered us their homes so we wouldn't have to drive back the four hours, but I made Monte say no because I wanted to be selfish with Eric. I had a right after two years of not seeing him. Wasn't it here at some other gate that I'd seen him off in just such a fashion?

After Eric had left, I was beside myself for two weeks until Monte called me out to the backyard one day, told me to pack my bags, fashioned a vacation up into Yellowstone to see the animals. I was fine on the trip, but I'd missed the week's mail from Eric and tore open his letter the minute we got home.

When he'd first left, his cards and pictures arrived home weekly, but then they started coming more and more apart. I thought that he'd probably gotten busy, made friends of families who asked him to stay for supper. You could always ask him to stay for supper and he'd accept. People commented to me on that. Friends at the market or stores would say "how nice it was to have Eric by last night." He was like that

A gate attendant swung open the door. I could have let my body go slack, but I was tied up inside like a ball of twine, holding nothing because I'd given my purse to Ann who was standing there holding four purses because the girls had given her their's so they could keep the sign up.

Monte leaned over to me and said, "Now, honey, you keep it together." I shushed him up quiet never taking my eyes from the door.

People came out furious like they couldn't wait to be off that plane. I looked past each one though, like they were just no one's you pass in a mall. But Eric finally came through the gate and the commotion around me just rose and rose, all my friends rushing towards him and Samantha forgetting all about the edge of her sign she was supposed to hold and it fluttering to the ground around my ankles.

And wasn't it just like me at the time to miss things? Like the fact that Eric wasn't wearing his garments and had removed his black nameplate that would have said Elder Eric Morris, proudly, like so many of the returning boys do. Wasn't it just like me?

Family History

Between the time Roy left for the canyon that morning and when he arrived back home, the outside air dropped ten degrees. Dark clouds marched their way up the valley and stacked themselves up against the mountains as if to create a billowy canopy over the land. Shafts of blue-gray rain fell softly over the city. It was a sight he knew he'd always love.

When he got to his door there was a note for him stuck between the frame. He paused for a moment and saw that it was from Eric.

Claire called down to him from her kitchen window. "What's it say?" He thought she didn't know him well enough to ask that.

Roy said, "It's nothing. From the electric company - a notice or something."

"Bullshit. We pay the electric," she said and laughed.

Bad choice Roy thought and looked at the paper which had Eric's number on it. He was a little distraught at the penmanship - the letters were slanted in opposite ways and Eric's circles were tight and constrained.

"Come up here for a sec. I'll make you something hot." Claire pulled open her back door, which needed oil.

Roy padded up the stairs not wanting to go, but if it was going to come out that he had a guy over last night he thought the sooner the better. Claire stood there in sweats which made her look thin. Her face was bright red from the cold and her hair was pulled back and tied in a ponytail.

"Come on in," she said and added, "coffee?"

Roy nodded and went past her into the living room. He hadn't seen their house yet and was impressed at how orderly it was - not a thing out of place.

They'd made an attempt at getting rid of the college collection of mismatched furniture and posters, which he'd assumed he'd inherited downstairs. The couch and love seat were a solid maroon except for a slightly dull pattern of gold that ran through the fabric. The house itself was pure fifties. The windows were plain and Claire had done her best to hide them with drapes to cover their sides and curtains that covered the bottom half of them. The kitchen's wood cabinets and handles were of a farmhouse quality that was extended by the tile over the sink and counters. Patterns of wheat stalks made them look like the tops of fields against blue sky. Roy sat down at a fifties style, light blue, naugahyde banquette as Claire pulled the table out. She took him in.

"Now he was cute."

"Who?" He knew she knew, but tried anyway.

"The guy you said goodbye to this morning."

"He's just a friend." The gigs up, Roy thought.

"You guys made a lot of noise last night for just being friends." She held up a bowl of sugar and went to the fridge for cream, placed it in front of Roy who sat there confronted by Claire's unbending honesty. Oh, what the hell.

"Were we too loud?"

"No, Chris and I were quite enjoying it. In fact, it got us going."

"Oh, man." Roy shrunk back into the banquette. Did he want to hear this?

"I'm impressed, though. Here in Happy Valley a little over two days and you've already scored. I want to know your secret."

"You're married."

"A girl can daydream." They both laughed and Claire sat down at the other end of the breakfast table and he told her the story of the night before. She had a knack for pulling information out of people. Outside, the sky grew darker and the clouds were as heavy as wool blankets; they finally reached his end of the valley. Rain pelted the front picture glass.

When he finally left her a couple of hours later, Roy slipped the piece of paper into a book by his bed where the phone was attached by a short cord to the only outlet in the place - another strike against the apartment, he thought. He took a shower, changed into warmer clothes, stared at the book with the number in it. He went out for dinner and left it behind.

Then he learned just how small Salt Lake could be. In the line at Crown Burger stood Eric and his friend, Frank, from the night before who rolled into Eric when he saw him and whispered something. Eric didn't respond and Roy wanted to turn and quickly go out, but they both had seen him, and went back to ordering. He moved to stand in line behind them because any other place would have been rude and, besides, there was only one other line working and that would have been too obvious a put-off.

Eric turned around. His hair was smoothed down on one side as if he'd just woken from a nap and his eyes were swollen to complete Roy's presumption. He wore a blue plaid shirt which lightened his eyes. Roy could almost see through them.

Frank moved up in line and left a wide gap between them. Nothing was said for a moment, but they both took each other in until Eric leaned over to him.

"I left my number."

"Yeah, I know." Roy said.

"Oh." Quick disappointment flashed over Eric's face. Roy internally cringed, was upset with himself for being so cavalier about it.

Frank stepped back. "Are you going to order or what?" He said.

"Just a sec," Eric didn't turn to acknowledge him, but rather fixed himself on Roy until he saw that there was nothing coming beyond the simple "Oh." Then he turned towards the cashier and without a single look to the menu board gave her his order, paid, and left to join Frank at a table.

Roy ordered and chose a table across the dining room, tried not to look their way, but found it impossible. He could tell Eric was doing the same. After his hamburger, he borrowed a pen from one of the cashiers and wrote his number on a napkin and added, "Let's call each other at 8 sharp tonight. We'll see who's first."

He looked back through the window to where they were seated after he'd handed the folded napkin to Eric and walked out. He caught them both staring at him and then Roy gave them a broad, big-toothed smile.

Frank

"You're not one to leave numbers," I said, my mouth full of onion rings dripping with fry sauce - a combination of thousand island dressing and ketchup without the relish that seemed to be unique to Salt Lake.

"I left work early to take it to him."

"You could do better," I reached over to take some more rings from Eric's plate. "I mean, you have done better. I've seen some of the tricks you've gone home with."

"Tricks?"

"You know what I'm saying."

Eric followed Roy with his eyes out to his car and watched him leave the parking lot and head up 1st South. He hadn't eaten much of the hamburger and the onion rings.

I was about to lose Eric. I could tell. I'd done my work. When he sees how pathetic the man across from him was - fry sauce at the corners of my mouth, a last bit of fried ring batter cluttering my fingertips, Eric will finally get disgusted and resolve to pull away if he can.

At some point in my relationship with these young boys, they begin wondering why they spend so much time with the likes of me - an old queen way past forty, fat. But I believe I provide a service to our young men and there will be another. The four calls per day and a rendezvous for dinner almost every night will diminish and I will go out and see another young boy one night at the bar who'll need my help. I went every Tuesday, Friday and Saturday and had the same old catty conversations about guys I knew - the ones sleeping with each other or breaking up.

When I met Eric, he'd been at his job at the trucking company over a year, not driving one like his father had thought he would once he started, but instead he was ordering parts which was a bore. He'd also started and stopped school at the university.

I met him just after he turned twenty-one when he began going to the bar. I was outside one night on the patio during summer. I commanded the bar like a captain, ordering drinks for everyone. I paid for Eric's drinks that entire first night and when I told him to come home with me Eric was too drunk to say no. We drove up into Emigration Canyon to my house, which is fully automatic: The garage door lifted with a touch of a button and all the lights, inside and out, flickered on once the door opened all the way.

My house then was was all blacks and grays and glass - floor to ceiling windows, leather sofas and chairs, light charcoal colored walls. I kept fresh, long-stemmed Calla Lilies pin-lighted so that their white cups shone as if lit from inside. I could see that it was all too much for Eric who flopped down on one of the couches and nearly slid off.

I stepped down into the wet bar and poured myself another drink, offered one up to Eric who declined with a wave of his limp hand, but I brought one over to him anyway. I studied him. He was probably wondering if I was going to want sex with him, or if there was some other ulterior motive.

"You're too innocent to have sex with," I said returning, the two drinks clinking from ice cubes. "So don't think I brought you up here for that and take that relieved look off your face. I've had better you know, but they cost me a fortune."

I sat down in one of the love seats and tucked my bare feet up under myself. I'd change into a loose shirt that hung over me like a caftan. I sat there with my gaze fixed on Eric.

"No, you just sleep this one off and I'll drive you back in the morning to pick up the car. Hopefully, the Mormon Mafia didn't take down your license number and call wherever it is you come from and let them all know you're a fag."

Eric was too drunk to feel real panic, but I'd remind him in the morning. I told him about them coming up from Provo and taking the numbers off the cars parked outside of the bar and running them to find out who they belonged to. Then they'd call the guys that owned the cars into the offices at Brigham Young University and kick them out of the college for being gay. Once branded, as if a scarlet G was burned into your forehead, you either moved out of state away from your family and friends or, as some of them did, take your own life.

"I can spot you guys a mile away," I took a sip and winced a little, "timid as birds most of the time. You can almost see the butterflies hatching in those little white bellies of yours. I try to be a friend." I put my glasses on to see him better. They enlarged my eyes so that they looked like large black holes, dark as olives. I never wore them to the bar out of vanity.

"Not wearing my glasses to the bar makes all the boys that much prettier." I shifted in my seat. Eric stirred. The outside sprinkler came on, the wind rose, a branch scratched the glass. The drinks were slowly wearing off. Eric tried positioning himself higher in the couch, but he kept slipping and finally gave up, took off his shoes and laid across it with his head up on one of the soft, pillowed arms.

"I'll get you a blanket," I said and got up.

Before I came back, Eric was asleep. I shook the blanket out and let it fall over the sleeping kid and stood over him. Another one to fix, I thought, picking up his glass. I took a sip out of it, wanted to taste something of Eric, but he never drank out of the glass. I took it into my bedroom to watch a late movie and hope for sleep.

From that night on, Eric had let me take command of his education into all things homosexual in Salt Lake. I introduced him to several people, chose some clothes for him, but always letting him believe that they were his choice. He rewarded me with stories of sex with visiting skiers, businessmen, an occasional local. In fact, he'd thought Roy was visiting because he'd never seen him at the bar before and thought he'd be easy prey.

Because Salt Lake was so small, I told him that if his tricks were from out of town, it was less likely to get complicated after sending them back to their hotels, or leaving them to call their wives or boyfriends back home. He might sound like a slut to some, but really there was so much time he had to make up for. His chaste existence up until then exploded away that summer.

I also covered the fine details of doctors to see if he picked anything up, which he hadn't so far, told him about some new cancer spreading back east among homosexuals, kept him away from the truly scary guys at the bar. It was almost like being in school. All this new information I told to him - a guy he couldn't imagine anyone sleeping with, let alone having a relationship with.

For the first year he was in awe of me and what I knew. Then my mentoring started to wear thin so that now, staring across at him at Crown Burger, him hoping I'd use a napkin soon, I could see that he began to think of ways to exclude me from the details of his life. He started with Roy.

Monte Morris

A father wants to pass things along. I've spent nearly twenty years building up my trucking business. Built it from scratch with one small truck and using my garage for storage. After a couple of years I moved into a small warehouse, got a couple of more trucks off a loan. I began shipping out-of state my third year. It was nip-and-tuck there for a while and I made mistakes, so I wanted Eric to learn the business not from me, but at another place so he wouldn't make the same mistakes I did. I thought he could learn some new things along the way. So I called up Peter, this friendly competitor up in the West Valley of Salt Lake, told him what was up and asked him to see about hiring Eric. He couldn't offer a driving job just yet, he said, but he'd fit him in someplace. I was grateful. I hoped that Eric would be too.

I was as worried as my wife when he came home from his mission. He'd changed though he tried not to show it. I was going to get him started here at my place, give him a truck, put him on a route - easy like up in Idaho or over to Nevada, the close-by states at first. But he was after something I knew nothing about - not work, mind you. I knew where his heart was about that. Hell, he didn't really have a choice having come by the warehouse practically every day since he was born. He had it in him. No, this was different. I figured since I got a lot of good years left in me I'd let him do what he needed. Hell, he could go work in one of those ski resorts up there if he wanted, but I still felt a need to direct him a little. A father feels that doesn't he?

Then I got a call one day a couple years after Eric had left Salina from some stranger, said he'd seen Eric at a bar for homosexuals, wondered if he'd been to church lately. I don't hold much stock in the church - not as much as my wife - she's kind of nuts about it. Not in a bad way, but maybe a bit too much. I don't say anything because of how strong she feels. Anyway, this guy calls, tells me this information and then asks me how I feel about it.

Well, at the time, I didn't know what to feel. I wondered if Eric had made some enemies up there and this guy was just trying to stir the pot a little. Or maybe he was from the church and Eric got caught up in some misdirected investigation or something, I didn't know. I figure if Eric had something to tell me, he would in his own good Goddamn time. Ah, see, you made me cuss. I don't get into that because of all the cussing that goes on around here and I've made the mistake of taking it home with me and Laura threatening me with cleaning my mouth out with soap.

I got rid of the guy and after a few hours at work my mind shifted back to filling trucks for their routes. It's a personal thing, you see. I didn't shut it all out of my mind. I wanted to pick up the phone and call Eric. But I was a little afraid to do that. I had a business to keep steady for him. I didn't want to mess that up.

Can we talk about this later?

Snow

Roy took Eric's number from the book and set it by the phone. After dinner he came back determined to unpack the boxes, store away his clothes on a rack he built from plywood and bricks. The prospect of someone coming over, possibly staying for periods of time, put the pressure on him to devise some way of making a home out of what he was beginning to regard as a hovel, no bigger than a bear's den might be in some cave.

For two hours he kept his eye on his watch while he went from room to room. When it got close to eight o'clock Roy stopped what he was doing so he wouldn't be out of breath for the phone call. He didn't want to sound distracted, so he turned off the radio.

Outside, the rain was still falling with the temperature, which held the promise of the season's first snow. On his way home, his windshield wipers tried to bat the rain away, but the rubber had rotted. He knew he'd need replacements so he could at least see what was up ahead. In fact, it was so bad that he'd made a wrong turn and headed up E Street when he should have been on H. As he got higher, nothing looked familiar and it was dark, and the rain began turning into wet globs on the windshield. Finally, he got out of the car and searched for a street sign before he found out he was lost. When Roy made it home, he made a list of all the things he needed to do to winterize himself before he started work.

At eight, the phone hadn't rung, so he went and got the number and called Eric. He wasn't much for phone games and, in retrospect, thought how silly it was for him to instigate one at the restaurant. But on the first ring the phone was snatched up as if grabbed for on a last ring.

"Hey." Eric's voice came soft and sweetly from the other end.

"Hey, back." Roy relaxed and fell against his bed because there was nowhere else the phone would stretch to.

"You sound tired," Eric said.

"Wouldn't you be if you were up all night with some guy?" They both laughed, further cracking the ice of a first conversation after a first night.

"Luckily, I got a nap in."

"I wanted to, but I ended up trying to explain our night to my landlord upstairs. Apparently, they were all ears."

"Oh, no."

"She didn't buy my standby 'we're just friends' routine. We also turned them on."

"You've gotta be kidding."

"She told me!" Roy could hear Eric shifting, trying to contain his laughter.

Eric got control of himself, "Is that okay with you that they know?"

After a moment, Roy said, "Now it is, I suppose."

"You suppose?" There was a change in Eric's voice and it halted as if a piece of food had gotten stuck.

"Well, I'm not the kind of person that I want people to necessarily know my story."

A simple "Oh" came from the other end of the line. The mood changed dramatically and very quickly, which bewildered Roy who thought that the conversation had started off very well.

"I mean to say…"

"You're not out yet," Eric said, flatly.

"It's a topic we didn't discuss last night. We'd agreed not to talk about our families and that sort of stuff." Roy's voice changed too. Was it disappointment or fear? He decided on disappointment because here is where you begin to find things out that may not be agreeable. Or it shifts to fear because what if he finds out something that was on his list of unacceptable things? Roy had a few items on his list that included drugs and excessive drinking, or more specifically, mean drunks whose mouths begin to rattle off their true feelings who, in the morning, take no responsibility for what they've said. It also included people who lie because he was the kind of person who'd been lied to his whole life by his parents so that trust didn't come easy.

"Well, I'm not completely out either." Eric's voice was small, a bit of tightness in it, but it also had a tilt of 'I'm sorry.'

Roy was relieved, suddenly and completely. "So we can move on to other topics?"

"Yes, but we'll come back to that one." Then, against Roy's rules of engagement, their family histories slipped out of them, edited to be sure, because that kind of information is always held for ransom.

All through the conversation Roy tried to picture Eric, phone crooked in his arm, in his apartment on his couch (or so he said), one leg over the arm of it, languidly talking to him as if they'd known each other a long time. He listened for his breathing patterns, ones remembered from the night before, and how his consonants were sharp and clear as glass. Eric spoke to him in Spanish, Portuguese and for laughs, a mangled mess of both which he'd mentioned that he had to use in some parts of Venezuela. But mostly, his breathing because in-between their lovemaking he'd listened intently to the soft whirring of Eric's contented sleep.

Roy intermittently fell asleep towards the end of their conversation. Long lapses punctuated the conversation. Eric repeated himself several times. They made a date for the following night.

Later in the evening, Roy woke to find himself still in his clothes and the apartment lights still on. He padded into the bathroom, peed, removed his pants and shirt, laid them over the sink, closed the door and stared at himself in the mirror. He went back to bed and felt the cool sheets warm quickly as he fell back to sleep.

Someone knocked on the door.

Roy, eyes swollen from sleep, hastily pulled a pair of sweat bottoms on and opened the door.

"Come with me," said Eric, and Roy went out into the night.

They sat in the cab with the heater on at the top of the avenues watching the snow blanket the houses and the city beyond. The snow was floating now, buoyed by its cold and a slight breeze that interrupted its downward spiral. Eric had made Roy dress so he could be the first to show him the city in winter. He said it wouldn't last: that the first snow was only a temporary thing, but should be etched on the memory for its newness and for cleansing the city of all the detritus within the lives it held.

Roy was pleased. He didn't say anything when he got out of the cab and walked to the edge of the street to look out over the houses. Eric came up behind him and wrapped himself around him.

After several minutes Eric said, "I'll take you back now if you want. I just wanted you to see this." Roy shook his head. There was no light or sound except from the houses and city below: a dog barking, a car engine being started, but they were muffled so that they were indistinct, like distant conversation. Eric kept himself tight to him, but even that seemed lost to Roy who was just letting the snow fall around him, getting a taste of it and smelling the air.

"This is amazing," he said, "I've never seen so much snow falling in my whole life. It's like feathers." He stuck his hand out to examine the flakes, but the minute they hit his palm they disappeared and left it wet. He'd seen snow, but in the mountains he hiked in, and not in a way that he felt as if he could get lost in it or become invisible.

Eric nudged him with his nose against his neck.

"Let's not sleep together tonight," Roy said.

"I wasn't planning on it."

"Last night was so good, I don't want to trample all over the memory of it."

Eric turned Roy around, kissed him. Their lips were cold and snowflakes came down between them adding a wetness, which tasted good to him.

For the next few days, Eric was compelled to show Roy everything about Salt Lake. He tried to stay clear of Temple Square though Roy wanted see it. The Mormon Temple rose from its walls like a gothic cathedral at the end of the street. Its granite spires reached up like arms, and in the middle was the tower that held the golden Moroni statue, which the Mormon's believed would blow its horn when catastrophe struck. They lit it up the most because of its duty. Eric turned as if to get away from the Temple's hulking shape, and its shadow that fell over the street like an eclipse.

They walked up City Creek where the fall colors covered the road. It was late October. The city itself seemed as if it were burning from the red and yellow leaves that mixed and gave the impression that there were pockets of fire across the valley.

They went out to the Salt Lake that was high from two years of above normal snowmelt. The water threatened to spill over the interstate and continue across the salt fields that were being lost to flood. The smell was hard to take, but Eric wanted to show him how really quiet a place could be. He wanted to show him how he'd like to live someday - with barely a ripple of trouble or misspent emotion, beauty.

He took him to eat up in one of the canyons where they made pancakes so big they covered the entire plate. One was enough for anyone, but they both had two because they'd woken late that morning, and then the drive and it was one of the last true days of autumn so they felt like squirreling away food for winter.

In bed that morning, before they'd finally gotten up, Eric had his ear over Roy's stomach, which sounded hollow and watery inside. He turned and rubbed it lightly feeling the hair on his chin and cheeks.

"You should meet Donna," Eric said.

"Who's Donna?"

"We grew up together and then she moved to Vegas. She's got this great girlfriend."

"Ah, she's one of our kind." Roy brought his hand down over Eric's head and stroked his hair.

"I think she'd approve of you."

"I want approval. I'm a little needy that way." Eric shifted up in bed and covered Roy. Their bodies were the same length though Roy's was softer, pliant around its curves and Eric's was hard - muscles stretched over bones hard. Eric wanted to cover him like a blanket, warm, enveloping, but the cold of the apartment made him shiver so Roy pulled the comforter over him.

"When we were sixteen we sort of gravitated towards each other. She had this don't-fuck-with-me attitude that, I think, gave me a clue that she wasn't into guys at all. I could've been wrong, but it turns out I wasn't. She was what I would call voluptuous then, big bones, and a heaviness that hadn't blossomed yet, and these huge tits the guys made fun of. She was a bit of a bombshell."

"That's a Dad word."

"What?"

"Bombshell." Roy laughed.

"Well, that's what my father called her, but not in front of my mom. 'She's a bombshell, that Donna. You gotta watch out for those kinds of girls,' he'd say. Of course, we became best friends." Eric was still on top of Roy and now the heat grew between them, sticking their stomachs together.

"Is she still in Las Vegas?"

"Yeah, we're - or I'm supposed to go down in a couple of weeks for a camping trip. I already told her about you. She wants you to come." Roy kissed Eric hard to avoid an answer for a couple of seconds.

"I don't know what work is going to be like," Roy said, pulling away.

"Let's not think about that until tomorrow morning."

Donna

The thing about friendship is that it's all so fucking dependent on what you know about each other. Good friends know everything there is to know about the other. Great friends always leave one or two things out. You tend to leave out things you think your friend can't handle. It's like it took years for Eric to tell me he was a homo. Years! I knew from day one. But in Salina, you didn't talk about stuff like that. Not when you're a minority like I was - not being in the church and all. I never brought it up to him, even when we invited each other to our senior proms. I was a year ahead of him and needed a date and when his time came up the next year, we swapped. It was safe for us to take each other, and as much as we hung together people thought we were a couple anyway. Even our parents thought so. I just let that one ride until I left home after graduation. I didn't so much as touch another girl at school. Not that I didn't want to, it's just that it was too risky.

I guess Eric and I could have gone ahead and done it. One night we almost did, but then we came to our senses and stopped. It was partly the Mormon thing with him and I, frankly, couldn't see myself doing it with a guy, or more specifically, with Eric. I was curious to know what it would have been like, but I knew what I was back then. He was still trying to figure it out. He was distant about it. I suspected there was something he wanted to tell me, though he never has, not even to this day. Now I'm glad he didn't and never will. It must've been bad, though. I can tell you that much. I think Roy knew. I think Roy knew everything there was to know about him. Which makes me wonder. Was Eric a good friend or a great friend?

Twins

His first day on the job and Roy was exhausted. The whole weekend had been a crash course of the city through Eric's eyes. It was like coming into a new world. The snow hadn't stayed from that one night, but it left the city sparkling the morning after. Leaves froze and melting ice dripped from the trees and eaves of the houses. Their roofs steamed and a low ground fog rose where the sun struck.

It started that morning: Roy's feelings for Eric and for the city. It was as if a piece of him had been replaced or found. He didn't want to be too sentimental, but the two of them combined wrapped themselves so completely around him that he felt safe.

The city was a place on the verge of change, from extreme tradition rooted in one religion to one of factions. Neighborhoods took on the characteristics of big cities. Ethnic groups, the poor, middle class and rich were lining up their territories, but it wasn't as apparent as where he came from.

As they drove around, people were raking their leaves, putting in storm windows, cleaning gutters - fall chores. It was as if a collective voice had run from house to house and neighbors stood in their yards, leaning hard on rakes, taking breaks from the battles they waged against the mountains of leaves that had fallen from the heavy snow. Or they simply stood talking to one another - a sight that Roy wasn't used to because the people in Los Angeles were too busy, or hired gardeners to tend their year-round lawns. It was a profound change for him to see this: a city and its people working with the weather that befell them, made them stronger, held the city to some higher purpose. Maybe that's why the early settlers of this church had claimed the valley as their own

- the protection of two mountain ranges on either side, the distance it took to navigate the largest inland lake west of the continental divide, the ability to see strangers come up through the valley so that they had the chance to prepare. Roy felt a need to be here.

Leaving college, leaving Tim behind in Los Angeles, had been easier than he thought. The echo of it had worn off on the long drive up, first through the desert, then into the high plateaus and plains of Utah. Each mile created a sort of distance, a memory. His friends and his lovers might have been acquaintances now. It wasn't that he cast them off like a thing that is a nuisance, but with his friends he was closeted, and his lovers, distant. Nothing resonated with him during the past four years. Getting through college was what he did to become something: an attorney, teacher, doctor, engineer. He went to counselors in the sophomore year to see if he was on the right track, that the major he'd chosen was suited to him. Recruiting days on campus were like a circus; each corporation had a tent with banners, manned by smartly dressed men and women who stood out among the slovenly dressed students. They signed up for interviews the following day that were held in empty classrooms around campus. Only then were most students in ties, pressed shirts or dresses bought for the occasion. At the beginning of his senior year he searched the bulletin boards around school and ads in the school newspaper or hunted in the department job listings folder. He applied for several jobs and settled on the one in Utah.

During this whole time, Roy spent time trying to figure himself out. He tried to see his father on occasion to ask about things he was feeling; why there was a separation between what he wanted and what he would commit to, why he always fell short of happiness.

His dad, who had finally stopped dating, became tired of the routine of it, was still hard to get a hold of, or pin down. He figured the odds were better at horse racing than at falling in love again, so he could be found at Santa Anita during the winter and later at Hollywood Park playing the races, always alone, studying the betting ratios.

He was comfortable with that as if pulling on an old sweater or slipping into a pair of worn shoes. Unfortunately, the racing season came during the tax season, so in the summer he'd rent a little apartment down in Del Mar, near San Diego, and spend his vacation time at the track there. He made money. Lots of it. Every once in awhile he'd mail a letter off to Roy at school with a check attached to a group of winning tickets to prove to his son he wasn't wasting time or being frivolous because accountants, by nature, just weren't.

Before Roy left for Utah, he and his father met for dinner in downtown Los Angeles, which was halfway between their homes and where most of his father's freelance clients were. Roy and his Dad walked the city at night because it was deserted after office hours. They'd feel as if the whole of it belonged to them. They'd follow the skyways of Bunker Hill, the steps down to the Central Library, which was on the verge of decay, then into the bowels of the city towards Little Tokyo. They stopped in at the flower market. At night, it resembled the moment after a strong wind had shook a budding fruit tree of its petals which stuck to their shoes and made them slippery and fragrant. When they removed them at their favorite Japanese restaurant, they perfumed the entryway and made Mrs. Tiny - tiny because of her size, not her stature - smile every time they came in.

On such a night, shortly before Roy graduated, they found themselves cross-legged, propped up on ornate pillows of red and gold silk thread, a fringe of deep black surrounding them. The smell of green tea filled the room. The tatami mats creaked under their weight when they reached for the soup or the varied dishes they'd ordered that kept coming by way of Mrs. Tiny herself, who was instructed by Roy's father that evening to be a part of the celebration of Roy's graduation and birthday.

There was an air of nervousness about his father. He was too rushed during dinner and too solicitous towards Mrs. Tiny, who was trying to juggle his wishes against the incoming stream of customers which Roy could see through the cracks of the rice paper doors that were constantly sliding open and closed.

"You've got to be glad that you're almost done with school," his father said.

"The chicken is good," Roy said, avoiding another discussion about his education.

"You're still planning on Salt Lake City?"

"Uh, huh."

"Are you going to make a career up there? I mean, stay there to live?" Roy's father was looking at him as if over glasses, but with his fork full of noodles, a mouthful on hold. "Isn't it going to be hard trying to fit in up there with what you are and all that?"

"Not as hard as it is here."

"But there's lots of your kind here."

"My kind? My kind likes the mountains, likes to ski, likes clean air. It has nothing to do with whether I'm into guys or girls, Dad." And there was that pointed emphasis on Dad, again as if to explain to him once more that being gay wasn't a choice, but an aberration of want and need. Once he explained it to him like this: It's like going to the bathroom, Dad. You don't want to go, you have to. His father got it that time and so he stopped using the word 'choice' when he brought the subject up - which Roy counted as a small victory.

Still, the uneasiness. Mr. Bancroft waited until they couldn't eat any longer, until the small Japanese cakes were served to both of them and Mrs. Tiny had offered a small toast, and said her final farewell before putting her whole attention to her other guests.

He pulled out an envelope, the edges yellow and crisp from age. Roy thought it might be another check and more win stubs, but there was something different, a gentleness at how his Dad handled this particular envelope.

Mr. Bancroft wiped the table clear of watermarks and the spilled juices from the dishes. He grabbed another napkin just to be sure, and unfolded it and laid it gently over the table. He took out some small, black and white photographs - three of them - and placed each one carefully next to the other.

And there was Roy's mother, in bed, her white hospital dressing gown bunched up around her shoulders, her smiling, eyes glistening as if she'd been crying, holding one baby in the far left picture, two in the middle, and then only one in the far right photograph. Roy thought they might be pictures of him, but he knew that the middle picture was a thing that he'd been missing - the answer to a mathematical equation he'd spent years trying to solve. His father might not have existed at that moment, except his fingers were shaking so bad, and he was holding onto the edges of the two outer photographs, so that it was hard to get a clear picture of the babies and his mother.

A long silence followed. Roy reached out to calm his Dad's hands and took the pictures from the table to study them. At some point his father leaned in close against the table, crossed his arms and rested his head. He waited for Roy to say something, anything, but Roy was determined to have an explanation given to him. So he held onto the pictures and waited. His father lifted his head finally and reached for them, but Roy moved the photographs out of his way.

"Those are the only pictures of your brother. He died very shortly after I took them - almost before they lifted him from your Mother's arms, but I had no idea, I was busy taking the pictures, fiddling with the film."

"And Mom, did she know what was going on?"

"No, not until later. We let her sleep after the pictures. She was so tired. It took her twenty-two hours of labor to get you two out of her. When she woke the doctor came in to explain about a weak valve in his heart, that there was no way of knowing. I'd spent the time she was asleep in the emergency room with them trying to revive him, trying anything. Your mother never spoke of him, made me make the arrangements to bury him and we stood there, all the family around us, as if we were the only two there."

Roy gave the pictures back to him, but kept the one of him and his brother. He studied it. He wanted to see if they were the same, but the graininess and soft focus made it difficult.

"Why now, Dad?" There was a hint of anger in his voice. His father tried to keep the conversation low.

"I guess because, well first we, your mother and I, decided that it would be best you didn't know." Mr. Bancroft hesitated, "But when she left and it was clear that she wasn't coming back, I thought that maybe I would tell you. Then I got to thinking that you should get through your schooling, become who you were going to become. And now you have. Much more than I bargained for, but you are your own person now.

Roy's back stiffened, tension tightened his shoulders. He wanted to ask him: how would he know? How could he make that assumption when all his life he'd had this big, gaping feeling that there was something missing that he could never put a finger on; that he'd been trying to attach himself to something, anything since he could remember and now his father was telling him that that something could have been his brother, dead or not. Instead, Roy took the photograph and placed it in his shirt pocket, under his coat, as if it were a possession he wouldn't let go of. He took it out again, looked at it, replaced it, then brought it out again, held it between his thumb and forefinger.

Roy had telegraphed his feelings to his father who muttered, "I didn't know..."

"Did you name him?"

"It was Matthew, after your mother's father."

Roy studied the picture of the two of them. He imagined being held like that, feeling his mother's breath, the heat coming from her body, being aware of his brother as if they'd already begun sharing a connection. He said, "Roy and Mathew Bancroft. I wonder what it would've been like having someone know everything there was to know about me."

"Most people never get to experience that," Roy's father relaxed a little. "The closest you get to that is when you get married, but even then you don't ever really know."

They walked back to their cars in silence, the city now quieter than before, the lights in the buildings glowing, as if keeping awake for ghosts. They stood at their cars looking at each other. Roy extended his hand - they never hugged - and his Dad took it, held it hard as if he wanted to remove it and take it with him so that he'd have some piece of his son, but of course, Roy let his fingers loosen, signaling the end of the handshake.

"What are the chances that a man loses a wife and son?" he said and then got in his car. Roy wanted to do something for him, but didn't know what, so he kissed his fingers and placed them gently on his father's window as if giving him a blessing.

Part Two

"I still believe Eric will turn up some day, come in down the road driving that big semi Monte gave him to work with. I still believe that. I have to."
Laura Morris, Homemaker

"Fuck. Will you turn that thing off for a sec?"
David Bancroft

Peter

I don't know why I kept Eric from driving my trucks for so long. There was something about him that I didn't feel was right. I know he had just about as much driving experience as anyone I had under my employ because of the work he did for his Dad, but there was just something I couldn't pinpoint. I knew though that if I didn't put him on the road soon, I'd lose him. I'd had reports that he was really bored with the computer stuff.

So I went to look for him and found him in the trucker's locker room sitting with Kyle, one of our other drivers. Kyle's wife was expecting so he was playing it close to home and hanging out. Eric was on a break. He was wearing one of the white polo shirts we'd made up for the employees. There was a picture of a large, crimson red semi, the words Trailines Trucking on the side of the long cargo shells, slanted forward as if on the go.

I asked Eric to join me in the yard. I could tell he was a bit nervous. I had to laugh a little. I pulled us both up along side the brand new Peterbilt the company had just purchased. It shone so bright I put my shades on. It was one of those new sleeper numbers with the wind bevel at the top and a slim, but comfortable bedding area behind the seats.

I just started shooting the breeze with Eric, toying with him a little, talking about stupid stuff, nonsense. He just kept looking over at the truck, taking it in, not really hearing what I was saying. That told me he was ready so I made him follow me around the truck. I started pointing out the new features, told him the improvements that were made.

Eric took it all in. I pretended to jot down notes on my clipboard, but I was mainly watching his reactions. He was smiling a lot. I pointed out that the color of the truck, candy apple red, was brand new for a Peterbilt semi. The sun shot off the cab and white cargo hulls and illuminated the other, older trucks next to it as if its newness would enhance them. We walked clear around it. I could tell that he'd never seen a truck like this up close. Not even at his father's, whose fleet was aging, and in serious need of some of these newer trucks that were more user-friendly to truckers.

I asked him if he wanted to jump up into the cab. The controls were polished chrome, free of grimy fingerprints, the smell of diesel hadn't yet permeated the leather. The knobs bore the same markings I think he was used to, but there were more refrigeration buttons and levers, lights for the sleeping cab and a new stereo with cassette player and speakers mounted over the bed.

I pulled myself up on the passenger side, "Well, will this about do it for you?" I scooted into the seat and threw the clipboard up onto the dash where it clattered against the window. "I could tell you were getting a bit antsy doing all that computer stuff."

"I'm gonna drive this?" Eric was dumbfounded. "Why am I getting a new truck?" He asked from the back as he checked out the comfort of the sleeper, bouncing a little.

"Luck of the draw."

"No, really."

"It's only yours temporarily. We're waiting for Ben Northrup to come back. Actually, we're begging him to come back and trying to bribe him with this thing, but he's throwing a bit of a fit and this truck needs to start making money for us."

"Won't the other guys be mad?" Eric came back to the driver's seat, punched a few buttons, and threw a couple of levers.

"Yeah, I guess they will be, but I don't want to get them used to a good thing and then start griping when I have to take it away. And, from what your dad told me, you have more hours than most of my guys anyway. At least you'll know up front you don't get to keep it - not saying that you can't work towards something like this, but there you are."

I told him he could take it for a few runs in a couple of days, that we still had some work to do on it and get it registered. I also told him to find a girl or something to go with the first time out in case there was trouble. The weather was shifting into winter and I wanted them on the route to Cheyenne and then on over to Denver where the air would just now begin frosting the windshields, making the engine a little sluggish to turn over in the morning. I could tell that Eric's head was spinning. I just hoped he didn't get too attached to the truck.

Trucks

Just as Roy began dozing off in the heat outside of Baker, a huge semi went barreling past him like a sonic boom and shook the cab of the Blazer. It woke him and he pushed up in the seat as he watched it go by, it's chrome bright, the wheels kicking up pebbles that flashed off the grill of his car. He was on a downslope passing an emergency truck ramp. His foot lifted off the gas and the car slowed down to a crawl compared to the truck. Other people passed him on the right. He kept his eyes on the semi because it was the same color and look of Eric's truck - the one he drove for work years back.

Roy remembered when he got that truck and the night Eric asked him to join him on Veteran's Day weekend because Roy could have three days to be on the road. Roy said yes with a slight tremor in his voice, unsure of being held hostage all that time. He was not especially fond of driving. He'd only been in the cab of a truck like the one Eric described once. Looking down from the seat to the road made him feel as if he were falling off a cliff and that made him nervous. He liked to have a buffer between he and the next car, but on this truck, the only buffer was a slim bumper that only guarded against flying bugs and the occasional roadkill.

Eric arranged with Peter to take the weekend route leaving late Friday afternoon. They'd be on the road through two sunrises and three nights, driving from Salt Lake to Denver then through Colorado Springs and back home.

Roy drove out to the trucking yard after work, left his car among the idle semis which made it look insignificant and lonely. Eric thrust his hand out to greet him, shouldered Roy's duffel bag as you would a sack of potatoes.

He whispered, "I'll give you a good smack when we get on the road." He led

Roy over to the truck, threw the bag up into the cab, picked up the clipboard off the step.

"So this is home for the weekend?" Roy followed Eric who was inspecting the truck's parts, wires and chains that held everything together.

"What do you think?" Eric looked back at Roy.

"I'm up for an adventure, I guess." Roy stopped to peer under the cargo hull. "Man, a car could fit under this."

"Which means we don't have to worry about traffic. We'll just go right over them." Eric laughed, delighted that Roy had come.

"So what are we taking to Denver? I hope it's not hazardous waste." Eric went around the back and opened the wide doors as if he were opening the gates to some ancient ruin. They swung back and revealed boxes upon boxes on top of wooden palettes that had been hoisted up by forklifts one at a time and pushed into position.

"Lo and behold… computer parts." Eric sprung up into the back end and took a number off one of the stacks of boxes, wrote it on his clipboard. Roy saw something new in him, as if having a vocation now, doing the thing he wanted to do, changed him.

They'd been together a month. Claire invited them up for dinner with her and Dennis after a few weeks of "all that noise downstairs." At this point, Roy would spend a few moments a day with her and she'd ask about Eric as if asking about the weather - casually and uninterested - but Roy could tell she really wanted to know.

He tried to tell her about Eric, but he came out shadowy and fragmented. Roy realized that he hadn't really learned much about him after all. They were just having sex it seemed, great sex, but just sex. They never talked about their families or what they wanted or how they would fit into each other's lives. Roy was afraid to bring the latter up just yet. He didn't know how sure the footing was in order to ask him. Which is why he decided to go on the route with him, otherwise he wouldn't have the chance to be with him or to get out and see the country that he was fitting himself into.

Eric bounded down from the inside of the cargo hold, handed the clipboard to Roy who studied it because it was all so new to him. He swung the doors closed which creaked and groaned and then, with a great clanging metallic racket, came together and sealed. Eric locked the doors down, threw a bar across the back, chained that and then slid two levers into holes in the base of the truck.

"There," he said, wiping his hands on his jeans, "that should hold those things. A couple of more safety checks and we're on the road."

"You've been doing safety checks?"

"Have to," he said, "when we start out and at every checkpoint or weighing station along the way."

"How many of those are there?"

"A couple or more every state. There's no free ride. Plus they want to know if your load has changed from what you've started out with. That way they know if you've been up to no good. Have you been up to no good?" Eric clapped him on the shoulder. Roy was edging back a little from wanting to go. Eric brought them between the trucks, turned Roy around and into him and kissed him.

Roy pulled back. "Jesus, what if someone saw that?"

"You don't think I looked around a bit before I did that?"

Roy knew that Eric hadn't, he'd probably assumed there was no one in the yard because of the late Friday and impending weekend. It seemed that he really didn't care.

When he finished the safety check, Eric showed Roy how to hoist himself up into the cab. He placed his hand on the hold, put his foot on the step and then pointed to the fuel tank, which had another step and then told him to pull up as if he were climbing a rock. Roy could have figured this out, but he knew that Eric liked to show him new things. He decided that he'd let Eric guide him through the weekend.

"Are you in?" Roy nodded and smiled. Eric closed the passenger door, checked the latch and went around to his side. Peter came out, introductions were made and Eric handed the safety list from the clipboard down to him.

"Be careful, we're still going after Ben." Peter yelled out over the engine, which caught easily, but startled Roy a bit by its power. It eased into a rumbling idle and Peter knew that Eric let it go longer than he normally would because he was there and Eric wanted to prove to him that he'd take good care of the truck.

They pulled slowly out of the yard and onto the road leading to the highway. Eric explained the controls to him, the buttons, how he made the shift by depressing first the clutch, then pulling a lever attached to the shifter and releasing them both simultaneously. He told him how he'd taken the truck out for a couple of short runs during the week to get used to it and how, during lunch, he came out and napped in the back to get used to the feel of the sleeper cab.

Roy watched him intently, wondered if he'd lose him to the road, to this truck which seemed to him to take on the qualities of another person, a third between the two of them.

The Road

As Roy traveled further towards Las Vegas, the radio switched to country music from a talk show where they were discussing the end of the Reagan era, and that of President Bush, whose first one hundred days in office were essentially a shambles after he raised taxes. When he'd gone over a rise it was replaced by some high-pitched woman, lovely voice, singing about a new found love which was a relief since most of them were about lost loves. Roy didn't automatically change the station because the sound of the music was faintly familiar. Instead, he turned the volume up, tapped his other hand against the window rail, remembered the voice from a number of years ago in the cab of Eric's semi, the two of them singing clumsily along, trying to figure the words out a beat before she actually sang them.

Roy and Eric had come out of Salt Lake and into the high, flat plains of Northeastern Utah on I-80. Islands of snow surrounded them like ice flows. Ice dust swirled behind cars sending glittering crystals into the air and the large windshield of the truck. Roy took it all in.

A burgeoning ski resort was passed on the right. The runs were etched into the mountains from where they were, the hills scraped away as if they'd given up the trees themselves. Eric was testing the sound system, turning the fader control so that the sleeper filled with music. But then the details of the music were lost and so he switched it back, balancing the sound again between front and rear and leaving it essentially how it was to begin with.

Their voices hit the same notes together as if they were in the same choir section. Roy harmonized with Eric, swinging up and down the scale trying to catch him on some of the notes, but Roy stayed with him through the song and when it was finished, he stretched across the cab to Eric. More for finding out something new about him than anything else.

Night came as they were passed Coalville. Everything turned shades of blue; the river that ran alongside of the highway was darker than the land itself, which had turned the color of cobalt. The trucks headlights threw a large swath across the road and to the sides, but it had the effect of giving Roy tunnel vision so he closed his eyes, slid down in the seat and rested his head on Eric's lap and fell asleep.

When Roy woke from a change in the rhythm of the truck, Eric asked, "You hungry?"

"Very." He saw that Eric turned off the highway and into a large truck stop that was fairly empty save for a few parked trucks, lit by amber globes around their edges. They idled off to the side of the small country that was the truck stop. The diner, itself lit up in neon and fluorescence like a beacon or the gates of heaven - and maybe it was to road-weary truckers after four straight days of driving - stood in the middle, like an island, between rows of pumps.

"Why don't you go inside and grab us a table while I give this thing some gas. It won't take long." Roy climbed down and paused to get his sea legs for a moment before making his way to the diner.

He found a table with a large window and was able to watch Eric move around the truck. He looked as natural as a mother with kids in her kitchen. Another trucker came over to admire the semi and they stood talking for a moment while Eric filled one of the tanks. A stream of jealousy filled Roy for a moment. He wanted to be as interested in the truck as that man was, wanted to talk to Eric as if he knew the difference between engines, wanted to understand their gear ratios and torque so that there'd be another thing they had in common. But it passed when he saw Eric finish filling the tanks on both sides, and swing the truck around to add it to the collection of other semis. Eric came through the door smiling, again adding, with his hands, to the dark stains developing on the thighs of his jeans.

Roy looked around the café and noticed the menu was pretty much written out on bright neon stars and circles scotch-taped to any spare surface. Bold letters introduced meat loaf, lasagna, a thanksgiving-like cornucopia of turkey, stuffing, mashed potatoes, yams and green beans.

"I wanted our first meal together on the road to be special." Eric said and laughed.

"Which special. It looks as if everything is special here."

"We'll order one of each."

One of those hand-bells rung and soon a waitress came around the edge of the counter that had a row of vinyl seats, red with flecks of gold, attached to it.

She saw them after she eyed the heaping plates of food under the heat lamps. She said, "Christ, I didn't see you, I'm sorry boys. I'll be right there, you'll see."

Roy said, "If I were to say that she fit the stereotype, would I be wrong?"

"There's a million of those women all across America." Eric said.

They both watched her stack the plates up her arm, grab a couple of butters, pour a coke and carry it all across the diner to a table of truckers. "You gotta love 'em because they put up with a lot of shit."

"I can imagine." Roy said.

"No you can't, but you'll see." Eric said, a little more seriously than the last and Roy felt a little sting because it was another thing he really didn't know much about.

The waitress came at them while she dropped off dishes into a black bus tray, put up a bottle of ketchup that needed refilling, and grabbed a couple of menus out of a box by the cash register. She handed the menus to them and looked Roy and Eric over as you would a thing in a store. She might have wanted to squeeze and thump them because she said, "You boys are so fresh. Where'd you come from?"

Eric said, "Salt Lake City."

"You're going to Denver."

"How'd you know?" I asked.

"You're in Rock Springs, it's the weekend, not a whole lot gets shipped North this time of night so it must be Denver."

"He was asleep most of the way here from Coalville." Eric said apologetically.

"Then make him eat right," she said as she left. Roy watched her go and noticed white sugar and flour streaks across the rounded back of her black slacks and her white tuxedo shirt poked half out of them. The strings to her apron swished back and forth like a cat's tail as she walked. He thought that maybe there were things that you shouldn't call attention to when you reach a certain age, but he didn't say anything to Eric who, he could tell, was smitten with her.

He opened his menu. He noted that it was mostly about breakfast: Eggs any style, bacon, hash browns, twenty kinds of omelets, crepes, waffles, pancakes, the three varieties of juices - tomato, orange and apple - steak and eggs, burgers and eggs, ham and eggs, the list was many and varied. Something about breakfast at ten in the evening didn't appeal to him so he looked back up on the walls to see if he could hitch his appetite to one of the food stars.

After dinner, they climbed up into the cab and into the sleeper. Roy was stuffed with the meatloaf while Eric's stomach adjusted to the Thanksgiving dinner. And because they couldn't possibly refuse dessert from the waitress' descriptions, they both worked over a country-sized slice of chocolate cake with white icing and vanilla ice cream dripping with chocolate syrup. Now the sleeper felt cramped and Eric tried to fit himself in next to Roy whose stomach could be heard over the din of the other trucks.

Eric removed his jacket, slipped Roy's coat over his shoulders and threw both of them over the back of the passenger seat. He removed Roy's shoes, slipped his socks off, placed them inside the shoes, and undid his pants. He pulled each leg of Roy's jeans off slowly, folded them and put them at the foot of the sleeper. Roy helped him remove his underwear by lifting his hips. They never took their eyes from each other. Eric had no desire to see Roy's body - just his face because it was there that he could see everything he was doing.

Roy reached up and pulled Eric's shirt over his head and wiped away a smudge of grease from just above his elbow. Eric sat back on his haunches in the dim light, which grew darker as he pulled the half curtains closed. From there they made love by touch. The sounds of the truck's generator, the soft rumble of it, gently rocked the men together.

When they were finished, Eric brought a soft blanket, given to him by his mother, up over Roy's wet body so he wouldn't get cold. He leaned into Roy who'd fallen asleep, and wiped away a drop of sweat from just above his eye. He got dressed and went to the driver's seat, turned the engine over and took them both towards Denver.

Because the world is flat near Denver, and because the sky was clear of clouds, except for a few sifting themselves together over the Rockies, Roy could see the skyscrapers and outer buildings of the downtown area miles from the city itself.

Eric kept the cab warm. When Roy woke he sat up in the sleeper and peered through the curtains. The passenger seat was littered with candy wrappers from sour balls that Eric sucked on to avoid sleep. Eric noticed Roy looking at them.

"The yellow ones work the best because they're the sourest of all."

"How long have you been driving?" Roy asked.

"About six hours straight. I'm trying to make it to the shipping yard before I have to fill up, but I don't know...."

"How far away is it?"

"On the other side of the city from where we are. Luckily, there's no traffic on account of it being Saturday and early to boot." He reached back and stroked Roy's face. "How'd you sleep?"

"I didn't wake up once which is a first for me. I've gotta pee though."

"Yeah, me too. I'll find a truck stop."

"Do we have to eat there?" Roy reached his head through and bit Eric's ear.

"Put your clothes on."

When he got dressed, he scooted over the passenger seat and slid in. Now, he had the whole view of Denver, it's glass buildings reflecting the sun coming up over the land as if being lifted by a force that propelled it up and over the horizon. But it was only the truck's progress towards it that made it seem like it was rising unnaturally fast.

On his right, the Rockies pushed up from the basin as if forced by their own might. The peaks were jagged like that of a saw with some of its teeth missing, and there was a lack of rolling hills leading up to them which caused the mountains to look like pieces cut from construction paper and glued onto a bright blue background by the hands of a child.

It was clear enough to see the wind blowing off their edges and giving the mountains a sort of translucent, white halo, as if they were placed there by God, himself, and been given the distinction of being saints.

Roy sat in awe of the range of mountains and Eric was so moved by his reaction to their beauty that he drove past two truck stops, through Denver and made his way to their destination without saying a word.

At the shipping yard they were offered coffee and juice, and showers in the bathrooms the company installed for truckers. Two forklifts scurried over to start removing the wooden palettes. They moved like robots over the shiny concrete floor, their lights flashing like police beacons and their incessant horns loudly beeped and echoed through the warehouse.

There were eight other trucks lined up against metal roll-up doors. A small wiry guy in a hard-hat, worn brown leather coat and gloves that seemed impossibly large for his hands had guided them to their position. He seemed like a man with an awesome responsibility placed on his slim shoulders. Eric watched him from his rearview mirror as he positioned the truck so that the doors of the cargo hulls would open up inside the warehouse.

Eric was exhausted. He'd forgotten how, when he got to his destination point, his body would collapse under him; Those days driving for his father receded too far into memory, but now his exhaustion was called up to him like a dull ache from the past. While he waited for Roy to finish showering, he fell asleep in a chair outside the bathroom door.

When the truck was emptied, Roy and Eric climbed back in. There was a load to pick up across town, but not for a number of hours. They had time to fill, so Eric suggested a trip downtown so that Roy could get out and look around while he slept.

They pulled up in a side street off the main boulevard that coursed through Denver's mid-section. If you looked West, the mountains rose up behind the buildings. If you turned completely around towards the East, the long flat prairies began as if they were a sea of browned grasses that in spring, and early summer, turned to green.

Roy felt as if he were in the center of a map. He felt as if he could move off in any direction, or stay within his new boundaries - that of this world of traveling with Eric. He looked back at the truck from the corner of the boulevard, it's chrome and color muted in the shadow of a building. He thought of Eric asleep in any city of the country, the things he would see, the storms he would pass through, and the nights and days that would blend together as if in some dream. He also knew that this life was something he couldn't adjust to. He was a creature of habit and though trucking would offer up the routine of driving and destination, Roy needed now to create a home for himself, a stable life.

It was eleven in the morning, and their clerks were opening all of the stores, which were on Saturday hours. They lifted the iron guards and made them disappear as if by magic. They turned the open signs in the window and Roy watched them and nodded at a few. He walked into a flower store. A woman was cutting the bottoms off the stems of a group of white irises. He looked around and saw flowers arranged by color, the brightest in front, the darkest towards the back. It had the effect of making the store seem deeper than it was, but the refrigerator doors in the rear reflected all of the colors back at Roy, so when he noticed his figure standing there, it was as if he were part of an impressionistic painting. He stood in the center of the floor, aware of the clerk, but lost in the fragrance of the flowers, and of the memory it evoked of his night with his father at the Japanese restaurant.

For the first time, he didn't feel as if he were missing a part of himself, but rather he worked the idea of loving Eric over in his mind, like you would a problem to be solved that held no right or wrong answer.

"Can I pick you out some flowers?" The woman came over, wiped her hands on her apron and smiled. She was an older woman, gray around the edges with a sharp triangle of it in her bangs. She wore khakis and a heavy, blue printed overshirt with silvery buttons and a brooch in the shape of a turkey with a pilgrim hat.

"I'd love some, but we're traveling."

"Where from?" She scratched her forehead with a work glove.

"Salt Lake City and now over to Colorado Springs."

"That's a nice drive, but in the winter it can be treacherous."

"The weather's holding it seems."

"You've been lucky, though a front is on its way in." She went back to her cutting table where stacks of flowers were waiting to be pruned, bunched and put into the plastic tubs of water arrayed around her. She saw Roy watching her. "I usually do this on Friday," she said, "but my daughter's been ill and I had to close yesterday. She usually helps here, so when one of us is down it makes it harder to stick to the routine of things."

"I'm sorry to hear about your daughter."

"Oh, it's just that winter flu starting up. She'll have it, then I'll have it, then we're done for the year." She broke off the loose leaves of some lillies. "You said you were traveling with someone, no?"

"Yes, I am."

"Where is she?"

Roy paused a moment and wondered if he should lie, then decided against it. "He's asleep in the truck." She saw something in him that moment and went into the refrigerator case, pulled a red rose from a bunch. She took a bottle of water, squeezed the handle and sent a cloud of mist into the air and then waved the flower through it. She attached a small tube of water to its stem. She handed it to Roy.

"Here, give him this. Men love flowers too, you know, though they'd never admit to it."

He was a little embarrassed, but touched and said, "Thank you."

"You have a wonderful trip and come back. I'll have a bunch of those waiting for you." She laughed and went back to her work.

"I definitely will," Roy said, holding gently onto the rose, its singular shot of beauty opening up to him like a thing that satisfies a need.

He wandered around the different stores for awhile and then stopped in at a bakery and had coffee and a roll. The women inside saw the rose and smiled at him. It made him self-conscious, but glad to have someone to give such a thing to. He was careful of it when he set it down among the morning newspapers and dishes, and when he went to pay for his breakfast. He wondered how the care of something as simple as a flower could make him as vigilant as a parent holding a newborn. Maybe it was how he felt at this stage of being with Eric: everything was measured against the past - and the future - the settling in as precarious as stepping onto a tightrope stretched between two unknowns.

Donna

I can't recall when I'd heard Eric so excited. I think it was fall when he called down to my house. Yeah, it was, because our garden went to shit and all we had left were these sorry little pumpkins that for some reason just stopped growing at about four inches. It was a little embarrassing because if you can't grow pumpkins, which are like weeds when they take off, then it's time to find something else to occupy your time. Anyway, Eric just got this truck at work - brand new he said - and took Roy on this route and when he got home he was all talking about it like girls talk about boys when they're thirteen. He went on and on about how they'd drove straight through for three days, made love in the cab over and over, watched the sunrise together from a turnout in the road. It was all so romantic and disgusting at the same time. I wanted to beat the crap out of him, but I was happy for him too. I could feel his spirit so high through the telephone it infected me and my voice began to rise - as it does when I get excited - and I could barely keep still.

Amanda finally yelled down the hall for me to shut up, so I went outside on the patio, which was still letting off heat from the afternoon. I began talking to him as a conspirator, voices hushed, talking over each other as if planning for battle. We'd been talking so low that Amanda couldn't hear anything and then she got suspicious and came to the sliding glass door and looked out at me, my head bent, hand over the mouthpiece. Eric was still talking about the weekend they had and it got positively X-rated which I didn't mind, but Amanda wouldn't have approved. I can tell when she's upset with me 'cause her hands go to her hips and, God help me, she looks just like a double-sided teapot when she stands like that - all disapproval glaring at me. And what do I do? I laugh and then she gets madder like she did and I had to hang up on Eric and follow Amanda into the bedroom, or wherever she went off to and try to make her see things my way, which she did after a spell.

I'd never heard Eric so happy though. I'd gotten tired of hearing about that Frank guy all the time. 'Frank said this and Frank said that.' I told Eric early on that I didn't want to ever meet Frank. I just had my own thoughts on that. Who needs a fucking mentor on how to be a homo? It sounded like charm school.

The Fall Jumping Classic

One O'clock in the afternoon and Roy was halfway to Las Vegas. He felt the top of the Blazer, the windshield. Heat pulsed from both surfaces, the waves of it blurred and distorted the road ahead. He looked at the clock, digital blue, pulsing, a rhythm of its own to step into. He remembered Donna saying at the edge of the cliff, "Okay, now…. Synchronize your watches… 5:57:00. We jump at 6:03:00." Him standing there pushing the buttons on his watch, terrified of jumping from the cliff into the water. All of the campers, Eric included, naked, red lipstick drawn down their bellies; Amanda with circles around her nipples that Donna drew with care and then kissed each one of them in front of everyone. And there was Roy standing with Eric, fingers twined hard together, shaking, though the air and ground were still warm from the afternoon.

It was early November and growing colder in Salt Lake, but southern Utah was still warm, and in Las Vegas, warmer still. Eric and Roy had been dating for two months, had settled into a pattern of sorts - Roy working Monday to Friday and Eric just starting to pick up more runs. They switched trucks on Eric a couple of weeks into his driving for the company. Northrup came back, was presented the truck and didn't speak to Eric, not a word, when he drove into the yard on his last run with the new semi. Peter met him in the back, took the keys and handed them over to Northrup, who turned and walked away after telling Peter to clean out the cab.

Eric was disappointed for a few days, and Roy tiptoed around his feelings, massaged his ego a little. They took a couple of days off from work, and drove down to Las Vegas to meet up with the rest of the campers and to meet Donna and Amanda, Eric's best friends.

They passed through Southern Utah at sunset, went over rise after rise, the low hills, watched how those hills lost their roundness to become cliffs and jagged etchings of red rock. The trees, lately turning color, stood in bunches in the middle of farmed fields, the recipients of water from tiny streams that ran from late winter into early summer. The leaves responded to this cycle of winter runoff and summer dryness by turning red or yellow, or a cross of both - burnt orange tinged with brown.

Eric was lost in thought on the drive. When they'd passed the junction that would have taken him home, Roy wondered if he had the desire to swing onto the offramp and surrender into his family again. He watched Eric for signs of anger, (was it bitterness or disappointment?) at having to give up the truck so quickly, just when he was getting used to the feel of it. Eric knew he'd have to, but he got attached to it very quickly. Roy was good to him the last few days, and kept a wide birth. Other men would have tried to move in, reclaim him, make him respond to their own self-involvements and needs.

Eric made Donna push back the annual camping trip by a couple of weeks to cement his position with the truck, but he called her the night after it was taken away and told her that that weekend was the time to go. She made the arrangements, called the others that always went, made Amanda put her brother in charge of the restaurant, and she and Eric began making up menus over the phone.

They pulled up into Donna and Amanda's drive just past ten in the evening. They turned off in North Las Vegas, headed up into Henderson away from the lights, the gaudiness and fakery. Eric said, "I like Henderson because people don't know about it. Strangers think the people up here only service the hotels and are part of the underbelly of Vegas which exists only for tourists and gamblers, and the appetites of the sexually curious. You only have to drive the streets of Henderson to realize that it's a town of two and three-bedroom houses, some with pools, most with gravel lawns and cactus. I might move here one day if I ever decide to move from Utah."

They pulled into the driveway of a low flat home. Donna was the first to come out of the house. She was dressed in her baggy, beige shorts that hung down over her fleshy knees lined with the weight of her skin. She had a t-shirt on with some company logo over her breast. The calligraphy had worn off in the washings making it impossible to read. Her hair was long, a dark blonde, beautiful, Roy thought. Most short, round women couldn't get away with the length of it, but Donna always kept it just right and brushed.

Amanda followed behind her. She had squeezed into too-tight blue jeans, shoes untied, t-shirted also, but you could make out the name of her family's restaurant in white over dark blue; "Figaro's" rested on her chest, large as a billboard. Eric laughed as he got out of the car and both the women came and squeezed him between them.

"It's the sandwich ladies and I'm the meat," he said looking back at Roy, who still sat in the cab as if waiting for a truck to pass so he could open his door. The women would not let Eric go because it had simply been too long since they'd seen each other.

"Don't be afraid, Roy!" He shouted above a cacophony of squeals, screams and giggles from all three of them.

"God, it's good to see you." Donna had tears in her eyes because she was sentimental about things like homecomings.

"God had nothing to do with it." Eric said and kissed her on the cheek and then on the forehead.

"Then I'll thank Roy here if he'll get out of the car."

"You be careful with him."

"He looks like he can take care of himself." Donna went over and opened Roy's door. "Why he's a fine specimen. Shall we bottle him up and keep him?"

Roy stepped out of the car, took Donna's offered hand. He might have been stepping out of a gilded coach, led by a handsome prince, but it was Donna - a woman he'd heard a lot about.

"Amanda, what do you think?"

"He needs a shower and a shave. I'm reserving my judgment." She winked at Eric. "You know where it is."

"Well then, let's march his ass in there," Donna said, hoisting two duffel bags out of the back seat and pushing the two men towards the front door.

In the stall together, which smelled faintly of bleach, the two of them stood facing each other. Their hands moved over the contours of their bodies as if they were navigating a strange, but familiar room at night. Roy was now beginning to feel as if he were a part of Eric, more than a lover, more than a feeling that he could express. He traced his finger down the bridge of Eric's nose, his upper lip, caught it on the lower lip and then dropped his hand down all together. He might have been exploring his lost brother.

Eric moved in to Roy who met him with his cheek, and then his mouth. They both started smiling. The absurdity of them standing together, in a shower big enough for one, and because the length of the drive had made them punchy, it made them laugh.

Roy sensed that his relationship with Eric had finally attained some validity by meeting these two, impossibly large lesbians, who loved Eric just as much as he was beginning to.

When they finished their shower and changed into fresh clothes, Eric and Roy went into the kitchen where Donna was making quesadillas, chips, salsa and guacamole. Amanda fixed drinks for everyone and carried all the dishes into the living room. Their assortment of pets were arrayed across the furniture, the floor and in chairs that seemed territorial to Eric so he pushed one of the dogs off the couch and stretched out. Roy sat on the floor in front of the coffee table waiting for the women to choose their spots: Amanda next to him and Donna curled up against Eric.

"David isn't coming and he wouldn't give me a reason," Donna said, "I don't understand it because for the past few months he'd been badgering me about when it was going to be, who was coming and all that shit."

"Should we call him now? See what's up?" Eric asked.

Amanda said, "I don't know. He's been acting kinda weird lately and sort of dropped off the radar for a couple of months."

"He's lost a lot of weight." Donna fed Eric a slice of quesadilla.

Eric, through a thickness of cheese and flour asked, "Has he been sick?"

Amanda said, "We don't know. Nobody knows, but he doesn't look good at all."

"Maybe I should call him."

"Who's David?" Roy was feeling a bit left out.

"He's been going on the classic since we started. He invented the jump, but Donna sort of took it as her own. Didn't you, Donna?"

"I don't know about that. I added a few twists." They laughed like conspirators.

"I shouldn't have changed the weekend like I did. David's okay, I'm sure he'll come next year." Eric saw Amanda and Donna look at each other. "What?"

Amanda took a sip from her drink and Donna sat up in the couch. Amanda's face said: "David wasn't going to make it ever again," and she wondered why Eric or Roy hadn't picked up on the reason for his sickness. It was the mid-eighties after all, and word had spread.

Amanda turned to Roy and said, "So, tell us all about you."

In the morning, the campers collected in the driveway. There was Jonathon, short, compact, balding a bit early for his age; Anne and Jackie, another set of small, thin lesbians who'd befriended Amanda and Donna a year ago at a gathering of women in Palm Springs; and Ken ("Kenneth, Goddamn it!") whom all the guys couldn't stop looking at, but who was going to require some serious alcohol to loosen him up.

Because of the change in weekends, they'd lost some of the regulars, though Jonathon was a three-year veteran. They were going to meet a few others at the

The Narrows, Miles Deep

campsite who'd be coming up later in the afternoon.

Roy and Eric emptied the contents of their car into the girl's van and climbed in for the drive. Roy could see the women's bodies spilling out of their captain's chairs, could see the damage they'd done to the fabric on the side of the seats. They seemed to bicker constantly; if one said white, the other black. It was never argumentative, and kind of fun to watch. He thought that Amanda had a militant edge to her, that in a crisis, she'd be the one to take charge, but she allowed Donna to handle things, and subverted her own energies into making her the decision-maker.

And in this manner she asked Donna, "How should we go this year?"

"Let's go up through town and then pick up the highway past that Arco station we use."

Eric, who was tired, lay down on the seat and put his head in the cup of Roy's lap.

Amanda looked back in her rearview mirror. "What's the matter with you?" she asked Eric.

"We stayed up talking last night."

"I bet," she said making a left turn onto a busy street.

"Watch the road," Donna said.

"I am watching the road," Amanda said, proving Roy's point about their bickering.

When they'd gone to bed the night before, Roy put his belly into the small of Eric's back. Eric brought Roy's hand around and held it to his chest.

"We haven't been careful," Roy said.

"It's a little bit late for that. You're thinking about David."

"Yes."

"Is this the first time you've thought about what we were doing?"

"No," Roy said, staring past Eric's neck into the black of the room, "I just don't really think about it. I haven't yet. Tim and I weren't careful."

"Are you worried?"

"Sort of, but I have this feeling that if it happens, it's meant to be."

"What is that supposed to mean?" Eric turned toward him until they were face to face.

"I don't know," Roy said, choosing words carefully, "I'm not going to try and get it. I mean it's sort of a calculated risk with you. I don't think you would knowingly infect me."

"True."

"And you haven't indicated that you've been sick…"

"True."

"And you're from Utah, for God's sake."

"Ah, the real reason I've been left unscathed," Eric said, pulling himself up in the bed, raising his arms and bringing them down his body. "I've been touched by the powers of Zion, and a protective sheath, much like an invisible rubber, has been placed over my body."

"Kind of like that." Roy laughed.

"But I've been ex-communicated, not officially, but it's bound to happen. The cloak of Zion will be lifted and I'll be left to my own defenses. Maybe I should become a Christian."

"But then it's all wafers and grape juice and not very much of it."

Eric lowered himself in the bed again, wanting the comfort of Roy, and the two of them shifted, brought themselves together. "I like it when you're inside me and there's nothing there but us and I don't have to think about it." Eric said.

"It's like being too young to know any better," Roy said. "It's almost like the first time you have sex and there's that excitement."

"Yes."

"Do you mind that we're not careful?" Roy asked.

"No." Eric lifted his head, stroked Roy's thigh, put his palm flat on his chest. "It's what I want."

"Your friends are nice." Roy said, dropping the subject.

"The best," Eric said and placed his head against Roy's chest. They talked into the night and stopped to listen to the desert silence of Henderson. Eric wondered what Amanda and Donna were doing, if they were tucked together like he and Roy, whether they thought about such things as they did. Later, he got up and looked in on them: a huge mound of body under blue sheets, a lazy cat with one eye peering from a corner of the bed, the softness of them and their collection of pets breathing the night air, the rising and falling. He went back to bed and woke Roy. They made love in the shadow of Zion, unprotected.

Amanda pulled into the campsite. There was a smattering of cars, a couple of Winnebagos and them. They left a note on the bulletin board at the Ranger Station for the others and chose the campsite by driving around and around until they all decided on the convergence of the best view, the best firepit and the proximity of the toilets (as far away as possible to avoid the slamming doors and squealing of rusty springs). It wasn't important to have the same camp every year, but to change so that there was at least something different, something to adjust to for the regulars.

They spilled out of their cars. It was still warm, and the lethargy of the road had soaked their bones. The camp itself was quiet. People had gone off, left their cars and tents to explore, take in Lake Mead. Some had brought boats to fish or get in their last bit of water-skiing before the season ran out.

Roy and Eric got out and began unloading the car. Donna and Amanda had brought the big tent, a large complicated affair of canvas and metal pipe that still took an hour to set up now that they knew what they were doing. Donna and Amanda set out to arrange their banners and flags, string paper lanterns from the trees. One of the banners said "The Fall Jumping Classic Begins Here," another, "Jump or Die." They did it mainly for conversation as the other campers were always strolling by wondering what it meant. It gave Amanda the opportunity to chat them up which she loved to do as if they were customers at her restaurant. She was never far out of her element. Donna would sit there and fume until she got a few drinks in her and then she was off to demonstrate by pulling her shirt up while the unsuspecting campers gasped and quickly went on their way.

As the camp took shape, Donna paused to watch Roy and Eric and how they worked.

"How do you do it?" She asked them.

"Do what?" Eric said, and pounded a stake into the ground while Roy pulled the edge of the tent tight and attached it to the stake.

"You've put that whole tent up without hardly talking to each other."

"So?"

"It's just amazing, really."

"Why's it so amazing?"

"Because when Amanda and I do it, it's like doing a science project and reading the directions, then we start to get mad and it takes us hours!"

Eric said, "It's not that hard, you know."

"I guess not, but, just the same it's the whole approach to it. Us lesbians are supposed to be able to do that stuff."

"But tent making isn't a required course, is it?"

"No, just the auto mechanic stuff. That way we can be predictable."

"Well, then, you are unique among lesbians – totally helpless in the art of outdoor camping."

They finished the tent and moved in; the boys on one side, the girls on the other. What usually happened was that everyone who came ended up sleeping in a heap so that there were legs and arms, heads, colored stocking caps, blankets of varying materials and patterns, the odd sleeping bag, looking like a mound of people and discarded hand-me-downs at a bazaar or flea market. In the country of lost souls, these people would be found, taken in, and finally, given the comfort of each other.

Donna

"He's okay, you know." I had pulled Eric away and we were walking down to where the campers with boats lowered them into the water. The ramp deepened into the lake and now we were both standing knee-deep in it watching the other people work.

"I know."

"I've been watching you."

"Yeah?" Eric pulled at his ear, a habit he'd had since childhood, "And what do you see?"

"You probably won't want to hear it."

"Try me."

I took his hand. "You know I love you, don't you?"

"And I you."

"I'm not being flippant here." I bent down and cupped some water in my hand and splashed it on his face.

"I know. You practically never are." Eric trusted me, was respectful, and I knew he wanted my approval after all though he'd never admit it.

"I've never seen you so quiet, so utterly at peace. You never question each other, and I know it's still kind of early, but you'd know, or I'd know, that you were still trying to work things out, but it's just not the case with you two. You seem to exist together. It's like you'll never go through that adjustment period that's so awful sometimes. With Amanda and me it was horrible."

"I don't think we've gotten there yet."

"No, you've skipped it." I wrapped my hand around Eric's, "Don't blow this one, Eric. I mean it."

"What is that supposed to mean?" He's suddenly hurt because it hadn't even occurred to him that he would 'blow it' or could with Roy.

"That was harsh, sorry," I said.

"Can you give me a bit of credit?"

"I've just heard about you and so many guys lately, it just seems…"

"That I can't control my dick."

I laughed, "Well, I'm sure you're fine at controlling it. I just think you might use it a bit much."

"She flings an arrow."

"It's just a thought."

"You're right. I have been a bit random." Eric walked out of the water and I followed.

"It wasn't a judgment," I said.

"I didn't take it as one. I took it as an observation."

"I'm not saying that Amanda and I are perfect…"

"You don't have to be. I wouldn't expect it."

"I just sense something with you two. A chance at something stable maybe." I studied Eric's face, which was held tight and controlled. I took another tack. "Maybe you're ready to settle down?"

Eric said, "I don't know about that. We'll just have to wait and see. The good thing is that right now there's no pressure."

"I don't want to be the one to put it on you," I said.

Eric turned to me. His eyes had filled and he bowed his head and said, "Thanks."

The Cliffs

The others arrived late in the afternoon. Dinner was already in progress and they were all on their way to a fine buzz from a concoction that Anne and Jackie created out of fruit juice and rum. Donna and Eric greeted them with cups and hugs. Introductions were made: Andy and Mike, boyfriends by default because they'd met last year on the trip and were pushed together by all who were there because it was inevitable and planned by Amanda. Johanna, who with Amanda, Donna and Eric, had been there from the beginning. She'd brought the ceremonial plastic flask of Baccanora, a tequila imported from a friend of hers at the border in Nogales, Arizona. It was pure and illegal in the states, and imported like contraband by her friend's father, who had a cattle ranch in Sonora where they made the drink; all of them were drunk by dinner.

The couples drifted off as the single ones stayed by the fire, watching the sparks drift up in the sky. When the pairs came back they went into the tent and pulled their blankets and sleeping bags together and fell asleep.

The following day they woke late. Donna and Eric made pancakes, eggs, and bacon. They wasted the day away reading or talking, or taking short hikes along the lake's rim, or on the cliffs. They caught up with each other or learned their stories. As the afternoon ended, they all gathered and walked the two miles to the lake, the jumping point, and removed their clothes.

And there they were on the cliff, Roy and Eric, fingers twined hard, bellies painted by Donna. Eric was breathing as if trying to catch his breath after a hard run.

Eric said, "Just hold tight, close your eyes and let me guide you. Just don't forget to let go when we're in the air. Okay?"

"Let go?"

"Yeah, just let go when we're over the water."

Roy didn't want to let go. He was through with letting go, through with casting off the things in his life. He wanted something tangible, a thing to enlarge him. Two months now with Eric and he was afraid he'd gotten too close (high?) too soon where Eric was just ready. Or was it ambivalence that he felt, broken only by the need to have someone, anyone next to him, needing him. Roy couldn't make up his mind about Eric. It was as if he'd reached some plateau, where he'd exist, launch himself into a new direction after awhile or jump off the cliff into something unknown like the lake, whose water was growing darker as the sun dropped like fire into an abyss across the horizon.

"You boys ready?" Donna came up to them, still holding her lipstick, the tip of it flattened, the red over her fingers, melting.

Eric nodded. He was concerned about Roy and turned to him. "You don't have to do this, you know."

"I know. I just have this weird fear of heights and jumping into an unknown thing."

"You'll be fine," Donna said, "We'll all be down there to pull you to shore, if nothing else."

"That's comforting."

"And I'm like one of those buoys you see out in the harbor," she said, "I'll be bobbing back and forth like a mad woman if you need something to hang on to."

The others were gathering at the edge. They'd grown quiet this year where in years past they'd be shouting and laughing at each other. Donna moved up against Amanda and put her arms around her, sweetly kissed the nape of her neck. They were aware of a change looming or possibly aware of the fortunes of their love. So Donna held her and Amanda reached back to stroke her hair.

Roy and Eric inched toward them. Eric pulled Roy along, coaxing him.

"Who's got the tequila?" Donna shouted. Jonathon held up the container.

"I think we should break tradition and start with a shot. I know I could use one and Roy here needs one terribly. Pass that shit over." So the bottle started down the string of naked people standing at the edge of the cliff, the sun now descending rapidly. Roy watched each head tip back and the bottle pass from one to another.

Eric still held his hand, but then he reached over and kissed him. There was something about being there in the open, about the lake, the sandstone, the community of people. He felt that he could do this and looked at Eric, who was smiling at him.

"Ready?" Roy asked.

"Yeah." Eric said. Then both of them ran the few yards and cleared the edge of the cliff. For a moment they were weightless, screaming, eyes wide open. Roy let go of Eric's hand, but they landed in the lake at the same moment, their bodies twisting in the water, surfacing, gasps of air, laughter as all of their friends plunged in after them.

Amanda

Our lives became a series of meetings. Our friend, David, who'd stayed home from the camping trip, died. His dying wasn't so much a series of little eruptions of sickness, but rather a short descent into hell. He was a Showgirl after all, he said, to Donna and me, on the last day of our visits, and to die with dignity just wasn't an option. All of the cast of the Follies Bergere showed up one day at the hospital and couldn't be stopped as they presented, "Hooray for Hollywood" for the entire fourth floor whether they liked it or not. They went so over the top that they had to stop because David fell into fits of laughter and shit his bed and started to cry from the embarrassment. But they still gathered around him, sequins, feathers, lamé and flashing silver. For a moment the room seemed otherworldly from the reflections off their outfits. David grew quiet and looked at all of them squeezed in around him; most of them hadn't seen what AIDS did yet, they'd only heard, and for a moment they went silent. I imagined them imagining themselves in place of David, but then one of the boys started singing Ethel Merman and an uncanny rendition of "There's No Business Like Show Business," and the room erupted again in celebration. For a moment I could see David forgetting himself. He was laughing again. It was Donna who cried, so she got up and left me to tend to him until she could get herself together.

I told her later that each one of them came and bowed in front of him and exited the room one by one as if they were on stage.

I caught them in the hallway on their way out. Their jubilation was erased from their faces and not a word was being said. I wanted to go up and tell them thank you, but I just didn't know what to say.

Donna and I worked hard to stay together. We had to. We spent hours at meetings in our small, but militant band of activists. She ran out of time to make me the dinners she used to make. Instead, we'd grab a quick bite at my restaurant or some fast food joint on the way to someone's house or a hospital. The casts of the shows around town began to fill with understudies, and then casting notices were sent out as if the army were sending out for new recruits.

I'd never been near a hospital until David, but now I know the maps of every one of them, though there aren't many in Las Vegas. It's always interesting that these last ceremonies for our friends became more and more outlandish, more brutal in the face of ugliness, because it's ugly what they, no we, are going through. Our cast of friends has all but disappeared.

Part Three

"There are things you just can't tell to a gay man, no matter how hard you try."

Frank Petersen

"Eric Morris? Well, he was a fine boy. I was sorry to see him leave the church the way he did. It is always a terrible thing."

Bishop Jack Souther, Salina Ward

Halfway

Roy watched the sun set through the rearview mirror behind him as he headed down the long grade just before a sign that read Zzyzx Road. The many times he'd passed that sign, he'd wondered where Zzyzx Road actually went, the thought that one day he would see just how far it took him came at him again. But he was late, had left work exactly at five, drove straight to the freeway heading out of Los Angeles and up, up into the mountains out of the basin, the smog, the millions of people. So the green sign that had darkened now to a black, whose letters reflected back from the headlights, leered at him as just another missed opportunity. If the day was his, and he wasn't late for Eric's graduation party, he thought he might have taken that off-ramp this one time.

The off-ramp into Salt Lake was littered with billboards. The ever-present Little America Hotel ad, which had not changed since Roy had moved to Utah, perched ominously against the railing, as if it were bolted to the side of it. It had the odd effect of being like one of those cheerleader signs that football players run through coming out of their locker rooms. If Roy and Eric aimed right, they felt as if they could have plowed through it to enter the city. They'd been driving for eight hours, up from the desert and Las Vegas, towards home. The lights of the city extended into the low foothills that gave the impression of a vast glittering carpet.

They went by Roy's and picked up a few work clothes then down into the flats of the valley to Eric's apartment. They were pretty much talked out and now the conversation was about work, the mundane things of their lives. It pleased Roy.

Pulling up to the apartment, Eric saw his dad's old car. He wondered if he was here, and had let himself in with the key Eric gave him in case anything ever happened to him. His father didn't know about Roy and Eric wondered if he should drive him home before his dad knew he was back, but as Eric was deciding, his sister came out of the apartment and ran to the car. He wondered what she could be doing there, this hour, this time of year, and not at home where she was in the middle of her senior year in high school.

Opening the door, Eric said, "Hi, Sam…!"

"So this is him?"

"Who?"

"Your boyfriend or whatever." Sam shuffled a bit, peered in at Roy who just sat there and took her in.

"Hey, wait…"

"The man you work for called Dad. One of his drivers said that one of his friends saw you two on the road somewhere."

Eric was stunned, he sat back down in the driver's seat, his feet splayed out on the asphalt. Roy reached out to touch him, but Eric shrugged him off.

"It's okay. Dad's not mad, a little surprised maybe, but not mad. I've been trying to reach you all weekend, so finally Dad got worried and just told me to go and that I could spend the night if I wanted to," she looked past Eric to Roy, smiled, shook her hair out, "What's your name?" she said.

"Roy."

"Hi, Roy." She turned back to Eric, "Can I spend the night?"

"Does Mom know?" Eric was shaken, but he got out of the car, reached in the back seat for some of the camping gear. "C'mon, Roy, let's empty the car."

"She doesn't have a clue. Dad told her he had to give something to you right away and the only way it could get here was by me. He doesn't think it would be a good thing to tell her right now."

"How'd you find out?"

"I sort of heard dad on the phone with him when I was working after school on Friday."

"You're so fucking nosy." He was angry with himself, but he took it out on her. Roy was still in the car and it angered him even more, "Goddamn it Roy, aren't you going to help?"

Startled and stung by Eric's anger, Roy said flatly, "Maybe I should go home. I can bring your car back in the morning."

"No, you're staying here."

"I gotta go check in with Dad," Samantha said, "He told me I had to when I got here, but I was waiting for you. Now he's probably throwing a fit. Do you want to talk to him? Maybe you should call him."

"No, tell him I'll talk to him later."

Roy watched her go back to the apartment. She had long, thin legs and was short-waisted, skinny, not filled out completely. He had a thought she was a late-bloomer, but he could tell she was smart.

Eric leaned against the car and Roy finally got out and went up to him. He put his hand on his arm.

"I'm going to kill that son-of-a-bitch Northrup. He probably got all worked up when he heard that."

"What do you think is going to happen?"

"Don't know, but I probably won't have a job tomorrow."

Roy feared that everything had changed then, they were halfway there. He tried to put a spin on things. "It could be they just have everything twisted up. You could go in there tomorrow and it would have all blown over."

"You don't know truckers. They have all day driving, letting their little minds stew over the smallest infraction by their bosses. It's not like they're actually engaged in thinking about world problems. Northrup has the smallest mind of all of them, but he's a madman who exists on no sleep, which makes him more valuable because he can do more runs. Think of all the time he has to let his mind spin." Eric lifted himself off the car and bent over to shoulder a duffel bag, grab a cooler, and then he turned and headed towards his apartment.

Roy understood now what his twin brother had known about being born and feeling the rush of air: light, a warm and loving hand, a breath, and then to have it vanish and be lost.

The chaos of Eric's apartment; the floor peeking out from clothes, sacks, furniture, books, maps upon maps, the laundry, out of the dryer, but now wrinkled and played out, was still inviting. Samantha had pushed everything off the couch and had presumably sat and watched TV the entire time she waited for her brother, for it was still buzzing with noise and chatter, one of those awful women-in-peril Sunday night movies. Roy looked at her and she stared back, or had been since he walked in the room. Roy put down the rest of Eric's things from the car. The camping gear could wait until morning.

"So, you're Roy," she said, swinging her legs up and tucking them against her cheek.

"And you're Samantha." Roy didn't quite know what to say.

"Eric calls me Sam. You can too if you want."

"Okay."

"So are you guys, um, together?" She was wide-eyed.

Roy guessed that teenager's interrogations were direct in some respects. "You could say that, I suppose."

"Man." She said, and smiled, "Mom's gonna freak."

"You're not going to say a word to her!" Eric shouted from the kitchen where he was emptying the contents of the cooler into the refrigerator.

"I didn't say I was." Sam shouted back, her eyes still trained on Roy.

"I just wanted to be clear on that," Eric said, putting his head up over the counter so he could look at Samantha. "Did you call Dad?"

"I already did. He's going to call you in the morning. I gotta leave really early to get to school. He said I could miss the first two periods."

"We'll take you to breakfast," Roy offered.

"How come he sent you up here? He could have just called."

"He said it was something that he couldn't just call about right out. He wanted to know for sure."

"Know what for sure?"

"About Roy," she said

Eric came around the corner of the kitchenette.

"I guess I'm his spy or something. But really, it would have worried mom silly if he came up. Geez, what are you gonna do?"

Eric sat and put his arm around her. "I don't know," he said, "We'll figure something out."

She snuggled up to him, suddenly tired, but Roy could see her mind working, trying to figure things out. She looked at him, looked away, then back at him. She was not sure now of what to say.

"How about we fix you up a bed here on the couch. You should get some sleep and we're tired from the drive."

"Where's Roy going to sleep?"

"With me."

"Oh, right." She pulled away from Eric. She seemed not sure of him for a moment.

"What?" Eric laughed a little. It was an awkward moment. Samantha got off the couch.

"I thought about this all the way up here from home and was wondering what it would be like, you know, my brother liking a guy. I always thought you and Donna would get together."

"Donna likes girls." Eric laughed.

"What?" Samantha said, shocked by what she didn't know.

"We just saw them this weekend, Donna and Amanda, her girlfriend." Eric was trying to jolt her a bit into normalcy, making it seem like nothing, but Samantha shook her head.

She said, with a finality that implied that she'd seen and heard enough for one evening, "I'm going to bed."

Eric got up and went down the hallway to a cupboard and pulled down a blanket and pillow from a high shelf. He came back and put them on the couch. "Here you go," he said, "Don't lose too much sleep over all this. It's really no big deal, you'll see." Roy saw that he was lying about that.

"That's easy for you to say." Samantha shook the blanket out and put the pillow at one end of the couch. For a moment, they all stood and stared at each other. She was waiting for them to leave so she could get undressed. Eric took the cue and pulled on Roy's arm.

"Goodnight, Sam." He said, and nodded to Roy to follow him, which he did, and went over and turned the light off. "Hey, Sam?

"Yeah?"

"Thanks for coming all the way up here. I love you."

"Love you back."

Roy stood at the door of the bedroom. Eric sat down on the edge of the bed and put his face in his hands. Silence fell over them as if they were waiting for a thing to break, or the next act, as in a play after a discovery is made and now the explanation has to be given.

"I'm sorry I snapped at you outside," Eric said through his hands, "You didn't deserve that."

"It's okay."

"Now we have to talk about all the stuff we've been avoiding."

"Yeah, but not right now." Roy wanted to put things off. Bringing up their pasts and the reasons for the things that happened in their lives now might be too much for them to survive. "Let's just go to bed."

"There are things you need to know and I don't want to lie here all night letting them run around in my head, because I've successfully put them in some pocket of my brain that I don't use." Eric was the practical one, and would want to get everything out in the open so they could go on, maybe not in the same way, but in a better way. " You have to understand why I can't tell my mother about me, or you, so you won't be hurt." Eric got off the bed and removed his shirt. He pulled his shoes off, then his shorts. He stood in front of Roy in his boxers.

"This is just me, Roy. I'm just a guy. We've done nothing but fuck for two months and had some good times."

"I don't know if we should start this." Roy was angry a little, and hurt. He wanted to leave and come back tomorrow.

"You don't have to say anything." Eric removed his underwear. "I'm just this person who is so messed up, and you've come into my life and I want to say I love you, which I do, and yet there are things I can't reconcile in my head."

Eric was quiet for a moment, letting the words, "I love you," sink in. He avoided looking at Roy, half expecting him to turn and walk away, but he stood there in front of him as if he'd turned into a pillar of stone. "What is it that you can't reconcile?" He asked.

"The fact that I was fucked by my stake bishop when I was twelve."

Everything fell away. Roy's intentions became artifice. Words disappeared into the very air and walls began going up. He had a thought to try and comfort Eric, but he didn't give him any sense that he needed comforting.

"And no one knows but you?"

"Yes. And I let him because I liked it." Eric didn't expect to be so clear-headed or unemotional when he finally told someone, but there he was, telling it to Roy like it was a piece of old business, or a thought about something he'd been wanting to tell him that he'd forgotten. Eric went to the top of the bed and turned down the sheets and climbed in.

He undressed thinking of some way to get out of this moment, the homecoming, and try to regain the feeling they had after the jump from the cliff, the remainder of the weekend, but there was no hope of it. He moved in behind Eric and hugged him. Roy put his hand on his forehead, whispered to him that it was okay, tried to quiet him, but Eric buried himself in his pillow and didn't say anything for a long time.

They both lay there. Finally, Eric turned on his back and said, "What am I going to do?"

"You'll figure it out. Just don't be in a hurry." Roy scooted up so he could see Eric's face in the dimness from the light outside which gave the sheet-covered window a ghostly glow. He touched Eric's cheek, felt the wet and wiped it away. Among the things Roy needed was a clearer view of Eric and now he had it: the hurt, the anger, the frustration, the self-involvement; the long list of religious sufferings.

"I had a twin brother." Roy said, unexpectedly, wishing to take it back, hoping it would escape the room. He felt that he'd taken the light off of Eric and swung it around on him, which he didn't intend to do.

"What was he like?"

"I don't know. He died just after being born."

"It must be strange knowing there was someone almost exactly like you. I sometimes wish there was someone who would be like me."

Roy sat up in bed and Eric put his head in his lap, felt the heat against his ear and temple, and put his hand over Roy's thigh. "Do you miss him? I mean I don't know if you can miss someone you never knew. I suppose you could in a phantom-like way."

"As crazy as it sounds, I do miss him. Even before my Dad told me before

I moved up here. I miss my mother even more because I knew her."

"Don't you know where she is?"

"No."

"What happened to her?"

"She left one day and never came back." The room emptied of sound, the night closed in and held them captive to each other as they fell asleep.

In the early morning, Sam shook Eric awake. "I've gotta go," she said.

"Let me take you to breakfast," Eric said, turning away from Roy who's back was now uncovered; the chill woke him.

"It was nice to meet you, Roy," Samantha leaned over her brother, gave Roy her hand. "I hope you can come down to Salina some day."

"That would be nice, I hope it'll be soon."

Eric shot Roy a look and turned back to his sister. "Why don't you at least grab some orange juice out of the fridge and I'll be right out."

"Okay," she said, "Bye Roy."

Roy nodded her way and watched her leave. "Maybe I'll stay away for a few days while you sort through the negotiations with your family."

"What do you mean?"

"Just then you looked at me like I'd made some sort of mistake saying that it would be nice to meet your family and see where you lived, when all I was making was conversation."

"Can we talk about this after Sam leaves?" Eric was delaying their first real fight. "I've got to get something in her stomach or all she's going to do is grab a couple of chocolate donuts on the way to the interstate."

Roy wanted to say more, but instead he lay down in the bed and turned away. Eric pulled sweatpants on and left the room.

Samantha

I was sitting on the couch waiting for my brother, feeling stupid. How could I not have known? And why didn't he tell me? He was different now. I mean, he was in bed with another guy like it was a regular thing. Of course, I'm trying to be all normal about it, but inside I was a chocolate mess.

When my brother came into the living room, he sat down next to me and put his arm over my shoulder. I said, "Last night you said I'd get used to the idea, that it was no big deal, but all I could think about was that it was a big deal 'cause Mom won't know, no one is going to know but dad and me, and that's not fair."

"There's other stuff I can't tell you, Sam, stuff I can't explain and the way Mom is about the church and how close she is to all that.... Well, it would just kill her."

"But you're never going to come home again."

"Of course, I will." He looked at me strange, like I'd grown something on my face. "You look so different all of a sudden. You look wiser and darker. I'd say you were growing up."

"Shut up." I said, knowing that I'd started experimenting with makeup in the last year. My face needed some definition I was told by the lady at the ZCMI department store. My mom and I had gone down to St. George to shop and visit my aunt for a weekend. My aunt told mom to let my hair grow out over my shoulders so it would make my face look longer. It didn't work.

My brother hadn't seen me since that Christmas because he'd avoided coming home. He'd made some stupid excuse and now I realize that maybe it was because of this thing with Roy, or that he'd see the same people, have to answer questions about his life.

I think he thought of me differently because I'd driven up to Salt Lake alone, which I'd never done before. Dad must have changed his mind about me as well, letting me venture out like that. He always thought I was too young for everything. He held me back a year in school because my birthday fell so far after the school year eligibility, refused to let me drive until junior year though I could have in my sophomore year, and then I had wait to have my first date. It wasn't fair. I was glad I wasn't there when dad told mom what I was doing. She must have freaked.

"It wasn't so long that I was in high school, what, five years now?" Eric turned on the couch towards me. "I had these feelings that I might be into guys. But because of where we lived I held it in. I had to, the church, mom and dad. Now I don't. I'm only learning what's it's like…" He stopped as if remembering something he forgot. "To love someone."

"Is that Roy?" I said, as I looked towards the bedroom.

"Yes. And I'm okay with it."

My brother got up from the couch and went to the refrigerator and got a box of Pop-Tarts left over from the trip. He loved Pop-Tarts. I watched him put one in the toaster as I folded the blanket and put it at the top of the couch. I went and stood at the opening to the kitchen.

"I like him," I told him, "kinda quiet, but I like that."

"Thanks. You're the second woman in my life to approve. Donna liked him a lot."

"What's her, um, girlfriend like?"

"Oh, she's great, too. As big as a house, and one of the best people I've ever met."

"I saw Donna over the summer at home. I guess she came up to see her mom who isn't doing so well."

"Yeah, she said she might move her down to live with her and Amanda. That'll be good, I think." The toaster rang. Eric pulled a jar out of a cupboard. "You want jam on your Pop-Tart?"

"No, that's what's inside."

"Yeah, I know, but I like more on top."

"Then it ruins the frosting." I took the Pop-Tart from Eric and sat on one of the barstools and started eating.

"Sorry about breakfast. It's the best I can do. Next time, I'll take you up for a Greek breakfast at Nick's. You won't have to eat for a week after that." Eric went to look in on Roy. I polished off the breakfast and picked up my stuff.

When Eric opened the front door, the air snapped at us.

"Sam?" he said, following me out to dad's Oldsmobile.

"Yeah?"

"It's important that mom not know about this. Promise me." He put his hand on my shoulder, but I couldn't look at him.

"I've never lied to her."

"I'm not asking you to lie, just don't say anything. Will you do that for me, please?"

"I'll try."

"That's all I can hope for," he said and hugged me, "You're not a kid anymore. You've grown up since I saw you last."

"Call dad before I get home. I don't want to have to tell him everything."

"I will. Thanks."

"Come home soon." I was in tears and ducked into the car because I didn't want him to see. I turned the engine over, flipped the heat on and adjusted the temperature.

"Do you have enough gas money?" he asked. What a dad thing to ask, I thought.

"Dad gave me some."

"Food money?"

"I'm not a kid anymore, remember?" There was a bit of edge to my voice. I might have been upset.

"We never got around to talking about you," Eric said.

"There's nothing to talk about, call me anyway. You know, you can tell me stuff."

"I will for now on."

"No you won't. You never tell anyone anything. You've always been this sort of mystery man." I appraised him, wondered if he'd open himself up a little now that he had Roy.

"I don't have a reason to be now."

"Good. I've gotta go."

I could see that he was saying, "Drive safe," but I closed the door and, for a moment, glass and steel separated us. I lowered the window.

"I don't remember you being at home much except when I was little. I kinda miss having a big brother around."

"Come up whenever you want to," he said and slapped the door of the car.

"Really?"

"Really." Eric said. I put the car in reverse, eased out of the space and drove away. I felt relieved to be leaving. Is that a good thing? I don't remember seeing him much after that because when he came home, I was busy and then left for college. I'd have given anything to be older so I would have known him better.

Monte Morris

Things don't turn the way they should. You would expect a father to be angry or hurt or questioning whether he'd done something wrong when a son tells him he's homosexual. I was so confused, I didn't know what to think, but Laura wouldn't have understood, much less heard it if I told her.

Eric called me the morning after I'd sent Samantha, that's our daughter, up to see him. It was a good conversation. Very quiet. I guess we were so busy trying not to step on each other's toes that not much was said. There were long silences and then I'd hear a, "Dad, Dad, are you there?" and I'd have to chime in that indeed I was. Don't think it was awkward, because it wasn't. It was just us trying to understand each other. I've gotta say he's a great kid and grew into a fine person, caring to the last.

Most things I've heard is that some fathers kick their boys out of the house, or never want to see them again. I wanted Eric to come home. Yeah, that's right. I wanted him home so I could see that he was okay, see what was behind all this.

Maybe it was a mistake to do what I was going to do. I told him not to go into the office or back to Peter that morning, that I'd give him a job if he wanted one. I said for him to think it over for a few days, make up his own mind about things. I did tell him about the new Kenworth, the miles of chrome, and how I was deciding on who was going to drive it soon. I was letting everyone take it out for a run at the moment, telling each one of them how I was going to slowly replace the whole fleet. You have to stay competitive to keep your drivers. I learned that from Eric and what happened with that guy who ended up finking on him.

110

Did I care that my son was homosexual? You bet I did. I just never let him see it.

Now I'm sitting here talking to you so openly about it like it was casual conversation. Maybe because it doesn't matter after all this, or that I've made my peace with it. My wife, Laura, will know now I suppose. She's got a right. I should have told her a long time ago.

Winter

When Eric came in to get his coat, Roy was indeed, pretending to be asleep. He went over in his head what was transpiring, and played the events as if they were on a tape loop, running over and over. For half the time they'd been together, Roy had been in this bed, never once feeling as if it were strange or uncomfortable. If a bed could have a personality, or hold a feeling, it would have been one of comfort, like that of a hearth, lit by a small, but warming fire in a cabin, in a stretch of woods, frozen by winter.

He wanted very much to get out of bed and into his clothes and home where he could sort things through in the couple of hours he had before work, but he lay there instead, waiting for Eric to come back inside. He could feel the cold air from the open front door snake through the bedroom and lick his forehead and hair. He burrowed deeper under the covers.

Eric's smell was now ingrained in his memory; like that of old earth and wet hair, aromas he loved. He would have liked to stay buried under the heavy blanket and comforter, warmed and loved for a few hours more. Eric did say the words last night, or was it something said in panic and not expressed in the measured way one might expect when it came time to say those words, "I love you," for the first time? Roy said, "I want to love you" out loud to himself to hear the sound of it. He also thought of the shortness of time, wondered if just a couple of months could engage those feelings in someone towards him.

Eric coming into the house broke his thoughts. He heard him in the hallway and then the footsteps stopped and turned back towards the kitchen. Roy waited a few minutes to see if he would come in the bedroom and to bed, but he could only make out the sounds of him opening the refrigerator, taking down plates, filling something up with water. So he decided to get out of bed and into his clothes and get ready to go home.

Eric came in from the kitchen. Roy looked up from tying his shoe. They looked at each other but didn't say anything. Eric sat on the bed and pulled his jacket off.

"I need to get to work," Roy said.

"I know." Eric shouldered his jacket to put it on again, but then he shrugged it off and it slipped from the bed to the floor. "Whatever happens, I want you to know that I meant what I said last night."

"Which part," Roy said, feeling stupid for saying it like that.

"The part where I said, 'I love you.'"

"Oh that part," Roy couldn't resist being flippant.

"It wasn't a casual thing." Eric turned to leave. "You're treating it like it was casual."

"No, I've been working it around my head most of the night and this morning." Roy stood and blocked him. "Was it said out of desperation because of your sister and family finding out? Or was it because we had such a great weekend and then real life sort of smacked you around a little?"

"That's unfair."

"It's neither fair nor unfair, it's just what it is, because I love you, too."

Eric said after a minute, "I should take you home."

"I don't want to go home."

"You have to go to work."

Roy considered it, then said, "I'm afraid that if I go, you'll go for good."

"Why would I do that?"

"A premonition?" Roy sat down next to him and took his hand.

Eric lifted Roy's hands and opened his palms. "I can't tell you what's going to happen, but the reality is, is that I'll probably be out of a job with no money and no prospects and a reference by way of Peter that I'll never be able to use. And in this town, word travels quickly."

"Do you have any money saved up?"

"Not much." Eric let go and fell back on the bed, sighed and draped his arm over his eyes.

"You could move in with me until you get something."

"That would be nice, but it's not such a good idea. It's way too early for that."

Roy stretched out against Eric, then said, "You're probably right, but, let's face it, there isn't much of a choice."

"You'll start resenting me."

"Resent you?"

113

"Think about it." Eric said, and moved his hand over Roy. "It would be great for about a week. We'd play house, and then the petty little things that bothered each other would start adding up because we were stuck together, and we hadn't had the time to get used to them with the escape clause of having our own places."

The smell of coffee wafted into the room. They might have relaxed into making love, but this morning smell broke the mood, signaled that it was time to start the day. Roy would be taken home. He'd go to work like a good soldier, but unable to concentrate on anything in particular, except whether Eric would be there when he returned home.

As they drove through the city streets, the remnants of fall lay wasted on the sidewalks and in the gutters. The trees had shaken loose their leaves and took on their gray winter pallor. The planters that burst forth with color in spring and summer now were empty, preparing for the bulbs' winter freeze. The air changed overnight. No longer did the smells of harvest linger, but rather of diesel and gasoline, the smell of machine, and the sterile, clean scent of dry wind.

Nothing of meaning was said between the two men, and as the car climbed into the avenues above the city, it was as if a spell was broken or had released its tenuous hold over them.

When he was alone in his apartment, having said goodbye to Eric in the car, Roy began to cry. He called in sick, took a shower and changed his clothes. But mostly he cried. He thought of his father, circling the fancy names of horses, walking alone to the betting windows, plunking down ten dollars on one horse, twenty on another, betting his life away, but with the calculation of an accountant. Roy imagined himself as his father, or his vanished mother, just up and leaving everything behind like she did. He didn't want to take either road, had promised himself that he wouldn't, but that morning he felt he was closer than ever to the fork and having to decide which way to go.

There was a knock at his door. He saw Clare's silhouette against the window's flimsy curtain. She confirmed herself with her voice, sonorous and deep as an oboe.

Clare shouted from outside, "Roy? Hey, why aren't you at work?"

He wiped his eyes with his wet towel, and threw it into the bathroom as he went to the door. "Coming!" he shouted back. Halfheartedly, he opened it.

"Are you sick? I saw your car and, well, it's past ten and I thought…" Clare waited for a moment before going on, or for an invitation to come in.

"No, and I'm not going." said Roy. He held the door and blocked the entrance.

Clare couldn't tell if it was on purpose, or whether he was subconsciously shutting off her entry. "You don't look very good. Maybe you're coming down with something. I could make some tea. That would be good."

"No, I'm fine really, I just need to think a bit."

"It's about Eric," she pressed on.

Roy didn't want her intrusion right now, but he couldn't muster up the energy to rebuff her with an edge to his voice, or a simple sign, perhaps some body language to let her know that now wasn't the time. He'd always been bad about letting people know more than he wanted to tell them.

So Clare came in, still hot from her run. He offered her water, coffee, juice.

She opted for juice and settled into the banquette and slipped a little on the fake leather.

"You're upset." She sat back against the seat, put her hands flat on the table as if she were about to say something definitive again, but then let her arms relax. Roy could tell she wanted something about how he was feeling. He moved back from the door and she took her cue to come in.

"My mother didn't think much of me, I guess, or she would have stayed." Roy angled his eyes toward the window, saw the soft light coming through. He turned to Clare, "She could have tried harder not to leave."

Clare took the tie from her hair, which fell over her shoulders, the ends of it still wet from the run. She touched his elbow. "What about your father?"

"Oh, he stuck around, but he was sort of gone too; at least he tried."

"Why did you stick around?"

"Because I kept hoping that someone would stay."

It was clear to him that Clare was at a loss for words, or comfort for that matter. So he let her sit for a moment while he got up and fiddled with the stove, opened and closed the top of it to see why it didn't light right off.

Clare said, "Dennis wants kids. I swear I'm not ready for them. Never mind that I don't want to be pushed all out of shape yet, but just the physical presence of them stomping around the house, leaving a trail of mess behind them. I don't know if I ever want kids."

Roy set the kettle back on the burner, lit the flame with a match, "Oh, you will," he said.

"I'm not so sure. It's a big thing right now between us. He wants them right after we finish our degrees. He's got two years to go and I've got one. Besides, everyone in Utah has a baby they're pushing around right now. It sucks just going out during the day."

Roy laughed and settled back into the bench.

Now he was glad that Clare had come over, glad for the company after all. He wondered if kids were going to be part of his picture, but he doubted it. His mind went from thinking about Eric, the underneath things he wanted, living together, working through a daily existence. He thought it was supposed to go hand in hand with a real job, settling in. Now that Eric was going to be on the road, there wasn't going to be that everydayness. Clare and Peter may not be able to decide on children, but at least they had the ongoing proximity of each other to discuss it. Maybe one of them would relent, maybe it would fester, or maybe it would just happen, an accident, a drunken night or early morning. And they will be happy.

He could already picture Eric's leaving. The difference this time is that he would remember it. He'd stand on the side of the road and watch Eric climb into that truck and sign off with a wave, the engine turning over and snow crystals swirling up in the air behind him as he pulled onto the road.

"Hey captain." Clare touched his hand, pulled his index finger out and held it. Roy came back to her.

"Somehow, I'm going to make it so that no one ever leaves me again.

Part Four

"The sky just opened up like, well, I don't know what it was like… it was like nothing I'd never seen before.
Dawn Turitt, Park Service Ranger – Zion National Park

"It was freaky, real freaky."
Tommy Brownell, Student – Southern Utah University

"I'll explain in the next segment what happened and why."
Bob Blumenthal, Channel Four News

To Zion

They packed up the Blazer, the tent, sleeping bags, cooler (stuffed so that Eric had to sit on it while Roy snapped it closed), water in two-gallon plastic containers, a gas stove, bottles of wine, a lantern. All of which was mostly provided by Eric who'd had it all sitting in the middle of his apartment when Roy arrived, waiting, as if he'd collected it throughout the week, thinking of the things to bring and then laying them out so as they wouldn't be forgotten. Roy had almost nothing to add save for his own sleeping bag and clothes, though he'd brought the wine – four bottles of red, a worn tarp, and a camera to record the weekend.

When he arrived, Eric threw his arms around him and squeezed, vise-like. Roy laughed, a little embarrassed by the show of affection towards him, and not a bit uncomfortable like he thought he would be. It was a moment he'd pondered from the time they'd made arrangements to go camping. He'd found out that Todd was no longer living with Eric; he had left months ago for reasons Eric hadn't elaborated on in their conversation. In fact, he dropped Roy's inquiry altogether in a quick burst of subject-changing laughter.

Then the awkwardness came up when they broke apart and looked at each other. Roy had tried to lose a few pounds, gone to the gym, but failed at consistency, where Eric looked better than ever, trimmed up even from his graduation party. His hair was freshly cut, and he was wearing hiking shorts and a t-shirt that fit him snugly. Roy felt a bit inadequate, picked up a piece of the camping gear and hid behind it, "Should we take these down to the car?"

"Your car?" Eric went over to the refrigerator. "Want something to drink first?" Roy nodded

"You think we should get on the road?" Roy was nervous now, his desires for the weekend were heightened by his own over-heated mind. He wanted to move things forward quickly instead of relaxing into the weekend. Eric closed the refrigerator and smiled, perhaps remembering things about Roy he'd forgotten, like his lack of patience, his desire to take control. For a moment they both stood there and Eric got quiet.

Roy let go of the sleeping bag he was holding. "You look good, Eric. You've been taking care of yourself."

"I've had no choice." Eric came from the kitchen into the living room and picked up the sleeping bag, which had rolled across the carpet. "Let's pack the car and get out of here." This was a thing that Roy remembered to let Eric do, so except for the cooler, which they carried down first, he made the several trips up and down the stairs, from the apartment to the Blazer, with the gear while Eric carefully, and neatly, packed the cargo area.

Eric drove and got out onto the interstate faster than Roy by taking a completely different route. Traffic was backed up by the Friday afternoon crunch of cars heading in the direction of the casinos which were now beginning to glitter as they set off towards Zion.

Once they passed the outer edge of North Las Vegas, past the decaying hotels that sat needy on the edge of the old strip, they climbed up from the basin where you could see the entire city come to light. Eric reached over and took Roy's hand. He placed it on his thigh and continued driving like it was something common, a thing that they used to do driving everywhere when they lived in Salt Lake.

Roy tried to focus on the remaining heat of the day, but his mind held fast to where his hand was. He tried willing his emotions away, though it was useless, so he bent his head down, let it pass, and finally settled into the drive ahead. Then Eric dropped Roy's hand for a moment, which gave Roy a slight panic and made him take his hand back, but Eric turned the tape player on in the car, and reached across and grabbed Roy's hand back and replaced them both on his thigh.

The miles disappeared in the dark up past Mesquite. There was an hour left to go before the Utah border and Roy remembered the terrain as a plateau with low grasses, red dirt beginning to course through the cutbanks, mountains off in the distance where Big Bend snaked its way through the open desert. But now it was dark in the cab and Eric had grown quiet; the tape switched directions automatically and Roy began to doze a little after driving all day from LA.

"One night , I came up this way with my gun," Eric said.

Roy pushed himself up, "You what?"

"I drove up here and took a road that's around here somewhere and went out as far as it would go because at some point it just stopped." Eric turned the music down and rolled his window up as if to keep the landscape outside. Roy was now fully awake. The air grew hotter in the cab, but he kept still as Eric went on. "Fall, last year. It was a warm day, but not hot. The wind was coming southward I know because it was coming away from the gorge, blowing up sand and scratching my face when I got out of the car. I was just standing there looking out over everything, seeing how beautiful the sky was because it was turning afternoon colors which, out here are pinks and light oranges and blues. The gorge opening was dark at the time. And I remember that I thought that if I could just make it through that gorge and up into Utah, I'd be saved and not far from my family, but the news that I was positive was so new, so fresh in my head that it clouded it. So I brought out my gun and put it to my temple. I was ready to end it out there in the open against God himself because how could any God have put such an ugly thing on this earth and made it pass among two people making love?"

Roy's heart spilled open. His body got hot from the news, and then he got scared because they weren't safe when they were together. He began to cry. "As you can see, I couldn't do it," he said, "I was standing there, barrel to my temple and I couldn't do it."

Roy was stunned silent.

"I came out here the afternoon I found out. I'm not sick, you understand. It was just a fever I had and then the test because my doctor said it might be a good idea. It's just that right now, the prognosis for my life isn't good. Look at everyone who's gotten sick. They don't last a whole long time."

Roy concentrated on what the headlights picked up: the broken yellow line, glittering asphalt, a mile-marker. He concentrated on the things that would take him out of the present.

"Say something, Roy."

"I don't know what to say. I've never known anyone who's been sick. You're the first." Which was fact. He had only read reports in newspapers and magazines about the disease. He'd discussed it among his friends, but the moment he'd set the paper down or they were through talking, he'd forget all about it because it hadn't concerned him. He wasn't having sex anymore anyway, but now he wondered if it was subconsciously brought about by all he'd read and heard.

Roy asked, "What stopped you?"

"From what?"

"From going through with it."

"A lizard," Eric said and laughed. "About five inches of lizard." Roy didn't

120

respond, only stared out the window at the blackness. "I was looking down about ready to squeeze my eyes shut and this lizard ran across my boot. It was barely light outside, but I followed it a little until it ran under a bush, but then I started thinking that if that little lizard could survive out here, why couldn't I? I mean look how hard he has to fight everyday to make it to the next. So I drove home, told Todd I didn't want to see him anymore, but he stayed a few more months. He tried to help and it wasn't anything he did, I was just different. I needed to figure out how to live all over again.

"How long have you had it?"

"Hard to tell. A couple of years?" Eric turned to Roy who was counting out the years since they'd been together. "It's been way after you, so don't worry."

"Does your family know?"

Eric shifted in his seat. "On my first trip back to Salina, I drove up on a weekend to see them. All I could do was sit at the dinner table, look around at each of them and imagine myself not being there and how it would be. I couldn't help it. Mom was looking at me all night."

Across the valley, the Gorge loomed ahead of them like a gaping mouth. They couldn't see it just yet, could only feel that it was there.

Eric went on as if needing to let it all out suddenly, now that someone was there he could tell his secrets to. "Before dinner I was slicing some of the vegetables and nicked my finger and for the longest time I stood there and examined the little drop of blood that came out. I was thinking what a powerful thing that drop was." He looked again at his finger, as if the drop were still there. "Mom saw me and I felt stupid, then upset that there was no way I was ever going to be able to tell her."

"I developed a routine of checking for a patch of purple skin or spots, dropped weight, a cold sweat. But nothing came. I thought that I could relax a bit, but then there was news of David, and Scott, and Ron.

"Work was worse. Some days I was so depressed I didn't get out of bed. If the phone rang, I rolled over to snatch it from the nightstand. I explained away my absences, promising to return the following day. I waited for the disease to take hold, like a serpent circling around me wondering if it should attack."

"And now?"

"Now it's sort of a secondary thing. I figure the time I have is what I have. Nothing more or less."

The two of them pitched into silence as the new information clouded up Roy's head and a profound sadness descended on him. He moved closer to Eric as if needing warmth.

Donna

For the longest time we didn't hear from Eric. We called. We stopped by. We asked after him to our mutual friends and then one night, Eric just showed up. It was like two in the morning or something. Amanda and I were tucked in together because it was unusually cold for December. I don't know why I remember this, but it was also before we'd thought about decorating for Christmas.

We'd long since given him a key to the house, but it was still surprising to find him standing over us on the side of the bed, naked. Somehow I knew not to say anything, so I lifted the covers and invited him in. Amanda and I separated and he slid in between us. I cupped my hand over his cold forehead and my tits squeezed against his shoulders. He'd never come over like he did that night, but I knew not to say anything and to just let our bodies warm him up because his hands and feet were like popsicles and he shivered into warmth like you do when you have a fever.

Amanda told me later that she'd kept her mouth shut because, quite frankly, she didn't know what to do and that she was awake the rest of the night because he'd soaked her shoulders with tears. I'd fallen right back to sleep accepting him as before; just like we'd always done.

In the morning Amanda got up and went to work. I slipped out of bed and watched her squeeze into the cab of her beat up mini-truck that she'd never part with even though she could afford better. I air-kissed her on her way out the driveway, closed the door and went back to the bedroom.

Eric was lying in bed, eyes open, staring at the ceiling.

"Good morning," I said.

"Look at my body." He pulled down the sheet. I looked at it. Nothing there but all of him, which I'd seen a zillion times before.

"Same old homo." I tried to shake the mood.

"No, I mean really look." He waved me over so I went. "Do you see anything? Anything at all?"

"There is one thing. One tiny, very small, in fact, very little... " Of course, it wasn't so I could say so without insult. "One itty bitty..."

"Goddamn it, Donna, look!" He turned his back to me and startled me into surveying his whole body like a map.

"What am I looking for?" I asked, "because there is absolutely nothing here but the usual."

"Shit," he said and got out of bed, pulled his boxers, pants and shirt on and walked out of the bedroom. Of course I followed asking him what was wrong, why the body inspection and stuff like that, but he kept walking and went out the door.

When my mom came to live with us, she told me that just before Dad died, they laid in bed at night and talked about me, moments they had together, their shared life. All the while he's gently patting her thigh, just letting her know he's there, still with her. Amanda has this thing she does to me. She takes her whole hand and rubs it down the nape of my neck and holds it there just so. We might be doing nothing, watching TV or something. But she just holds it there and somehow I know she'll never leave me.

What I feared was that Eric didn't have that. Todd had gone. I knew something was up with him, but I didn't want to confront him. I never thought it was my place to do so. We were good friends, he would have told me if something was up.

Yesterday I found a map of Zion in Eric's house and brought it here with me. It's the geological survey kind with all those contour lines showing how steep the mountains are and how deep the valleys can be. Here you can see the river coming down through the Narrows. Look at how windy it is, like a spastic snake, wouldn't you say? Look how far it goes, and how if you can imagine it, the river goes right off the page and into your hand if you hold the map like I'm holding it right now. If I had any magic in me, Eric would slip off the page and back into my hand.

Amanda went with the forest service guy to help search. He needed a clear idea of him. I don't have one anymore. It's that old saying about how you can never really know someone. Ever since he made me make a map of his body, I've been talking to people, searching out the truth of things. It turns out that a friend of mine worked in the hospital lab, saw Eric's name attached to some blood tests. I guess he didn't have a right to look, but look he did. So I found out.

Some information is not to be discovered by friends. It forces you to see things, makes you feel so Godamned stupid for not knowing yourself. The thing is, what would I have done had I known before? I'm from Salina. We didn't talk about hurtful stuff.

There was this place when we were young that we'd go hiking to. It was called Buzzard's Peak, and all around it was scrub. Back then we were small enough to climb under the branches and make our way to the top. On one side was our town, laid out on a grid like most towns in Utah; streets went north and south, east and west. On the other side was nothing but the desert as far as you could see. I remember him saying to me, "You know, Donna, we could just keep walking. We could walk all the way to the other side of the world if we just went this way." He stuck an arm out and pointed out to the vast emptiness of land.

I remember thinking how fantastic it would be because of all those colors: the reds and oranges, the yellow wildflowers and green shrubs. How fantastic it would be to disappear into such color. That's how I'll remember Eric - walking headlong into color.

The Gorge

After Mesquite, and after a long silence, Roy noticed the moon and how it shaped the looming mountains ahead. He remembered this part of the drive from his many trips to Salt Lake. In the day, the earth here was pink, but now it was blue from the bright moonlight. Few cars passed them and it was past eight-o'clock. They reached the mouth of the Virgin River Gorge and began the ascent into Southern Utah, going closer to Zion.

The highway follows the river close. As you climb higher, the river falls away into the deep canyon. Midway through, Eric pulled into the viewpoint where you could get out and look down to see the rushing water.

They both emptied from the car, pulled sweatshirts out of bags, and walked out to the edge to see if they could see anything. The only sound was of the water and the engine settling. The stars were like scattered, crystalline beacons.

From the edge, before the steep decline, Eric said, "It's not scary to me anymore. After awhile you sort of embrace it. I hope you can get there, too."

Roy went to him and took him in his arms. "I'll try."

"I can't ask for more than that," he said, "let's climb down. There's a fence down a ways we can go through."

They made their way down the dark slope where the wire fence was torn away by falling rock and held by the remaining chain-link. There were low shrubs; Roy smelled sage. It awoke him to possibility. His mountain legs came back to him and he sort of plunge-stepped along-side Eric towards the river-bottom where it was cooler from the current-pressed wind. Eric swung his arms up as he jumped down to the sand from the last bit of ledge. "It's good to see you again."

Roy felt his way down the slope, slowly. The loose dirt give way and the rest of him sluggishly followed. He tried to make Eric out, but could only see his shape. Bared branches tugged at his jeans, unsteadying him; sand filled his shoes. Eric's dark body kept moving towards the water. "Wait for me," he said, slipping over a rock, "I can't see."

"I'm right here." Eric stopped to steady Roy, who didn't quite know how to hold on to him. He fumbled his way towards him and fell into his shape. Eric caught him and laughed. Roy saw him finally, again as he'd seen him the first time: strong yet gentle. For a moment they were together, but then Eric pulled away, started walking along the river's edge. "I went kind of crazy after we split." He leaned against a large rock for a moment then continued. "I was just fucked up. And I never told you. The trucking job was an easy way out."

"I don't think it matters much." Roy said, catching up.

"I do. Come here." Eric stopped and pulled him in, hard. "I remember this feel, your weight." He was a calming force. "It's funny how those things don't leave you."

Roy adjusted to him, took a breath, was nervous. The cold air creeped into his bones and he shivered. Eric didn't let him go this time.

Roy traced his fingers along Eric's nose like he used to. Eric bent his head to meet the touch of his fingertips. He started to shake, suddenly crying, wishing the tears would go away.

"Remember how I told you about that Bishop? The one who I messed with when I was young?" Eric put Roy's head in his hands. "Remember?"

"Yes."

"I told you that I let him have me?"

Roy nodded.

"That was recklessness. So was getting infected. I threw myself into every kind of situation. I figured if I could fuck the Church, anyone could fuck me."

"What?"

"I was tied to those restrictions for so long, I couldn't breath. When I was found out it was like the sky opening up, fresh air. You were looking for some kind of replacement. I wanted to go nuts."

Roy pulled away. "Do you know who...?"

"No. Does it matter?"

He remembered entering him. On odd occasions he remembered how it felt more so than other men he'd been with. He thought about the word enter; was it a way into him, as if being inside him was a form of possession? Hadn't he learned that you can never possess, only enter, and only for a short time, and then pull out, a sort of leaving, like an emptiness that can never be filled completely. Maybe being inside him for only moments was enough and maybe not, but that was before there was any thought of protection.

Roy could now pick out detail and he saw the small wakes from the water cascading over the rocks. He picked up a pebble and tossed it into an eddy, saw the splash, then the ripple outward towards the bank. "I loved you so much," he said, "it took me a long time to realize that and I've never been able to let you go. And we were together such a short time, but that can happen can't it?

"Yes."

They were quiet a long time. Time enough for the frogs to start their singing. The two of them listened quietly so as not to stop the growing cacophony of song.

"Roy?" Eric lifted his face towards him and whispered in his ear, "I'm sorry."

Roy firmed his grip around his hand. He felt fall coming on, the snap of air, and thought he could smell it too.

Later in the car, back to before, Eric caught Roy up on the girls, his family. He mentioned that he really hadn't seen much of the girls, had sort of split from their familiarity. They'd taken on the duties as caretakers for several of their friends and he couldn't deal with it. Though he'd come to some impasse regarding his own infection, as he explained to Roy, he wasn't ready to see its ravages day in and day out. He felt a loss for their friendship, Roy could see it in his face, which was now cast in the blue of the dashboard lights.

"I never told my mom about me," he said, "but she found out in the usual way that she did. She interrogated my sister. Sam never could lie to mom." His sister, who was now known only as Samantha now that she'd grown older, had been at college a few years and had a boyfriend of her own. Eric talked of her fondly, how as conspirators they compared notes on men, their respective boyfriend problems.

"Samantha left the church too, you know." Eric said proudly. "She thought if the church wouldn't have me then they couldn't have her. That's what she said. Mom was upset, though, but Dad was all right about it. I thought it was pretty cool."

They came out of the Gorge suddenly, as if being wakened out of the deep chasm of a dream. It also had the effect of making Roy aware of a shift within him. He was filled with possibility, as though there was a new chance at a beginning for them both. He felt that void in him filling up, completely erasing the past four years. He'd set his own house right, listing as it had for so long. His father had a new woman he was seeing, practically living with. He no longer spent his days at the racetrack. Now he understood the fascination his dad had for the horses; how with each race, he put a part of himself on the line, tested his resolve against failure, but knowing deep inside that the odds for his success was borne of his ability at numbers, confidence in himself.

Roy righted in his bucket seat. He and Eric passed the border sign and Eric began to hum a little with the music, his favorite. "Yonder mountain, so high. I can make it all on my own. Roy joined him. Rolling river why so wide, sweep me up and bear me on." - glorious words set to music, harmonized, worried to perfection by a singer who knew perfectly how they fit together.

Laura Morris

I love my children. I love my husband. If I made a list for all those sorts of things to be grateful for, I'd have to attach it to the refrigerator door so I could write each thing down as it came into my head. I'd write down all the good things in my life.

I never imagined it different. I've lived in Salina all these years, known the same people, the same stores. It has grown a little bit. New people come down from the city to live and weave themselves into the everydayness of this place as easy as fitting a hand into a glove. The WalMart took the place of Everly's, the strip of fast food stores took the place of home cooking. It takes five more minutes to pass through town since they've added the two stoplights at the corners of Main and Topaz and Main and ... oh, I've forgotten the name of that street. I've always believed in the simplicity of this place. I thought that the hard things of a city wouldn't touch folks here, wouldn't touch me.

Small towns aren't for teenagers. They get restless with a place when they see so much available to them on the television. It puts things in their head and they see things we never much saw when we were teens. So off they go only to bring the nastiness home with them.

I loved my church. If ever there was a safe haven for me it was the ward that I'd been a part of for so long. The world can spin out of control and I could count on the constancy of our Saturday gatherings, Sunday services and my family around me every Monday. You can see the lighted living rooms all down the block on Monday evenings and I imagined families gathering to share stories, read from the Book. Those nights were the only nights that I felt Monte was part of the church because he'd make excuses to be down at the truck yard on weekends.

On Sundays, Eric was mine. Monte knew enough to leave that day clear for my children who I didn't allow down there. I would make breakfast special, worry over it the night before, and be up early to beat the eggs, whisk pancake batter, fry bacon, and cut the fruit. I've always felt that a mother's love is what she set to table.

I've been a fool. Sometimes I wish Samantha could lie to me, but her face gives her away every time. And I don't believe she would have ever wanted to. But she had to get away from me to find herself out. I believe Eric had to, too. That's the price I paid for truth. Two children who wanted nothing more than to get away from home. Samantha's home now, of course. She flew in from Boston where she's living with a man off campus. She thinks I don't approve. Of course, she's right, I don't approve, but who am I now... who am I?

Am I a woman who's lived her life keeping storms away by believing in something that fills a space, or is it something that you do because others think you should? Should a mother have favorites? Did I keep Eric too much for myself? Now that he's gone I don't think so, but when I found out about him and that boy, well, I had so many questions.

When the church let go of my son, I let go of the church. I took a job on Sunday's at the WalMart to fill the time. Monte and I went to the movies on Monday nights. The neighbors saw me after services stocking shelves, helping customers. At night I kept our windows dark.

Bishop Jack left the ward for service in the church offices in Salt Lake. He never came by after Eric was excommunicated. It was a complicated time. I fought for my son to stay in, but the Bishop was sure that it wasn't worth the trouble. Every little bit of trouble shakes your faith. In some people it gets stronger, but in me it grew weak.

I asked for a transfer to the WalMart in Salt Lake City. I called my sister. I'm going to stay with her for a while. I love my husband, but there are things he never told me. I'll leave soon - in a couple of weeks or so - after they've found Eric, or even if they don't. There is one thing you should know, one simple fact of me.

I loved my boy.

Zion

They camped between cathedral spires, under dogwoods losing their leaves. Eric showed Roy the way to his body again; it was exactly as before. They were careful. Afterwards they slept and in the morning, when Roy woke, Eric was gone. He panicked slightly, then heard the rattle of pots and pans and gravel crunching underfoot. He lingered in the cocoon of their sleeping bags and blankets and was glad for the sun's warmth on the tent. He reached up to touch its ceiling and a small drop of condensation fell. In the distance, he heard the faint rush of river, and closer, leaves flicked against each other in the wind. He gathered up his clothes and pulled them on.

Roy felt a deep sense of relief. The night had gone well. Eric made love to him in the same way he remembered - full of need, a rushing towards something, as if being chased by predators. He knew the specifics; Eric's clenched eyes, his quickening breaths against his shoulder, the long shudder of release and his patient coaxing for him to finish, last like he always had.

It wasn't until he saw Eric, searching in the cooler, the sunlight dipping lower into the canyon, rimming his body in gold, that Roy was caught in the worry of him. He fell back on his haunches and watched from the opened tent flap. He imagined seeing through him, past his shape, him not there. He wondered how he would love him if he were gone. Having known he was still here, still available during the past four years, made it easy for Roy to put off what he felt. Besides, another man could have come and filled the space that he kept for Eric. It never happened and now he was left with a sand-filled hourglass, counting down the years… days… hours?

There was the smell of frying bacon; Eric concentrated over his two-burner stove, the one Donna loved. He had his gray UNLV sweatshirt on, blue jeans, a baseball cap. "It's about time you got up," he said.

Roy waited a moment to take him in, "I lingered in the sack."

"Good. You needed to."

He stretched, looked around and wondered why there were so little people around. "It's pretty quiet here."

"Yeah, kinda strange, but this time of year is a bit tricky. It can be either cold or warm, but people don't really camp now. Only hardcore people like us."

He moved up behind Eric and peered over his shoulder to see the crackling bacon. "You've got the touch. Do you think you made enough?" The bacon was still in heaps and Eric carefully separated the slices with tongs.

"I had to buy a whole package and I've got other stuff for tomorrow morning."

"What's on tomorrow's menu?"

Eric turned and faced him. "You'll just have to wait and see." There was a moment: the togetherness, the break, then back to the task at hand. Roy sat at the picnic table and waited. In the waiting, he watched him work. And he fell into that space where a child sits watching his mother work to bring food to the table.

Roy's mother worked with precision. She'd slice the vegetables, dice carrots - she'd gone to cooking school to fill up that space created by his twin's leaving. He came into the world briefly, as a fly alights on a solid thing, only to find that it moves in the wind. He'd watch his mother work at the kitchen counter, shoulders hunched over. Always the work. He doesn't recall his mother ever sitting or taking a moment. In the short time that he'd been aware of her in an objective way, he remembered that she wasn't one to hold, or caress, or bend. The last time she'd held him in any real way was perhaps in the photograph that his father gave him.

It was in that other lifetime. When there was a sense of family, of love, the longing for it. When that sense disappeared, when the ground shifted underneath his mother's feet, he knew that she had no choice but to leave, because staying would have destroyed her. Her leaving made sense to him now.

He was afraid that he contained her sense of loss, but hadn't he found again the substance to fill that void? As Eric cooked breakfast, the smell of bacon grease permeating the air, taking Roy back to his mother's kitchen, didn't he see in him someone who could know him completely, as a twin might, or as a mother does in a child's first years before losing it to the world?

132

After breakfast, and after they'd cleaned up the tent, they drove to the trailhead of Angel's Landing - a steep climb with a guaranteed gorgeous view of the valley according to Eric. On the steep incline, Roy rested while he continued to climb. After an hour, his heart felt like it was being barely contained in his chest, and his legs felt rubbery and soft. He wondered if he could make it, but Eric came down and pushed him onward, coaxing him by telling him stories, lifting the weight of his daypack off his shoulders by holding it underneath while he walked behind him.

At the next rise, they stopped. Roy sat on a ledge, out of breath, "I'm embarrassed."

"It's just you and me up here." Eric handed him a water bottle. "You've always been a city boy with a country heart."

"I suppose."

"This is heaven - which I guess is why they call it Angel's Landing. You should see the view from the top."

"I hope to eventually." Roy gave a small laugh, as if the reality of climbing even two more feet was out of the question.

When they reached the summit and walked down the long slope of rock, Eric stood at its lip and surveyed all that he could see. He looked left up canyon and right following the river past the gates of rock, the campground and its decline into the desert beyond.

Roy was still trying to catch his breath, happy to be over the hard part and ready to just sit, relax and let the sun do its work traversing the sky. Eric sat down behind him and scooted into his back. "Remember the day we split?"

"Yes." He had played it over in his head a million times in the last four years. Eric had called him from a pay phone from across the Salt Lake Valley. He'd parked his truck and was waiting for a haul wondering if Roy could come meet him. On the way, Roy stopped at a flower shop to buy him a rose. He spent a few moments looking through the refrigerator case. It was a simple thing, he thought. He just needed one. So he picked out the largest red bud he could find. Its petals were just beginning to curl out. When he got to the cash register he saw a group of plastic-stemmed roses with silk petals. He looked at the rose he had chosen, then back at the bouquet of fake ones. Something about them stated permanence so he chose one and replaced the other back in the refrigerator.

When he got to the truck, Eric was waiting there, hair tousled, jeans greased black, the rim of his eyes red from sleeplessness.

"Climb in," he said. So Roy hoisted himself into the cab. "What do you have there?" He handed him the rose. Eric took it and smelled the fake perfume, it's too sweet fragrance cut the cab's smell of diesel.

Roy said, "I thought this one would last."

They moved into the back of the cab, made love and then Eric slept. Roy stayed awake. After an hour, the sun descended, raking its light across the buildings, the valley floor. Roy shook Eric awake. "I have to go."

"Stay."

"No. I've got to go." He quickly dressed. He had to get out of the cab, its protection, and its mixture of Eric, sweat and the road. There wasn't anything to say. The pull of the road had got to his partner: the wide west, red rock, the converging highway lines, and black space of night.

"What for?" Eric sat up, pulled on his crumpled shirt, stained pants.

"You and I are going different places and I can't be a part of what you want right now." Roy moved into the front passenger seat. He wrestled with the door and swung it open. Air rushed in. He jumped out.

Eric tied his boots and followed him out onto the gravel pitch and back to Roy's car, which was parked along side the road. "What do you want me to do?"

"I want you to get back in your truck and drive away."

"What?"

"Get back in your truck, Eric."

"You're fucking crazy. What's happened to you?" It had gotten to dusk, blue edged to orange on the horizon; dark behind and light ahead.

"I don't want to live your life and you don't want to live mine. You asked me to come all the way out here so you could fuck me and then be on your way."

"It's not like that at all," Eric shouted over the roar of a passing semi and the cars following it. Rushes of wind caught the words, carried them off like lost thoughts.

"Then tell me, what is it like for you?" Roy stared at him, came up face-close, the sun now making its descent over the horizon. Eric didn't say anything. "Go back to your truck, get in and go. You're late."

For a moment there was a wide gulf between the comings and goings of cars. Eric stood there. "Come with me."

"You don't want me to come with you. And I couldn't even if I wanted to." Careful, Roy thought. "I want to, but I can't."

"Come." Eric reached for Roy, but he backed off.

"Your life is just beginning. Go." Roy's look was final.

After a moment, Eric turned and went to his truck, took a long eye back, and disappeared into the cab. The engine fired and the gears locked into place. The loosening brakes squealed. The truck's heaviness pushed over the edge of the asphalt.

Roy watched it vanish. The twilight gave the white hull a ghostly glow. A wave of grief washed over him. It took him a long time to get in his car and drive away.

Eric pulled his backpack from his shoulders and unzipped a side pocket. He took out a worn plastic rose and held it in front of Roy. "Here. It's traveled a lot of miles to come back to you, but I want you to have it."

Roy thought that the world was constructed of terrible consequences. If he hadn't of let him go, would Eric not be facing certain death? If he'd only jumped in that truck and left his careful world behind could he have saved him?

It has taken millions of years for the river to cut the valley and the changes are too slow for the naked eye to discover. Roy had constructed his life to circumvent change, to be safe only to find that the one thing that made him feel safe he'd let go in an irrational moment on a highway in the middle of a valley he never belonged to.

He closed his fingers around the rose's stem, clutching it, wanting it to have real thorns to punish him. Eric closed his hand around Roy's. "Tomorrow, we'll hike the Narrows.

The Narrows

In the graying light, Eric and Roy found themselves four miles deep inside the Narrows. They had started early, rising again to the sun on the tent, putting together their daypacks for the journey. Roy was stiff from the hike, but he was anxious to get going, to see things he'd only seen in picture books: the swirling designs of red clay canyons, the shafts of light coming down in brilliant translucent curtains. It all turned out to be true. He stood in the middle of the river and marveled at the intensity of color.

But now, the temperature had dropped hard in the last hour and they'd both put on sweatshirts and windbreakers. Cold, they decided to turn back, but they were also hungry. Eric took a couple of sandwiches from his backpack, unwrapped one and handed it to Roy. In the middle of the river they ate, shivering because they'd stopped moving. Roy put his hand up to Eric's face and wiped a smudge of dirt away and then held it there. Eric bent into its warmth.

Thunder cracked miles away and a quiet rumble rolled through the canyon. A raindrop fell into the river and then more came down, dotting the still eddies and darkening the red rock walls in burnt umber streaks.

"We'd better get going," Eric said, stuffing the rest of the sandwich in a pocket of his daypack. "Finish that up and let's go."

Roy thought he caught a worried look in Eric's face and nodded. He ate quickly as Eric moved down river. It was easier going with the flow of water, but it also made it more difficult to navigate the shifting rocks underfoot.

Another volley of thunder, the sound of it was closer.

The two of them walked faster. Rain came down hard, soaking their hair, hiking shorts and windbreakers. The canyon walls dripped rain and it had grown darker as if dusk was falling though it was still only one in the afternoon. A slight wind came at their backs from up river. Roy caught up to Eric.

"What's happening?"

"I don't know." Eric said. He had his suspicions, knew that to be in the canyon during a rainstorm was dangerous, but he didn't let Roy think there could be trouble. Only Roy knew there was, but to confirm it was a different thing.

"How long do you think it will take us to get out of the canyon?"

"At least a couple of hours." Eric said, "If we run it could take less, but we could break an ankle or something if we're not careful."

"Think this'll blow over? Do you just want to wait it out?"

"We could if we found an embankment. There's one further down."

"Let's get there and then decide."

They continued down the river as the rain beat on them. At first, they didn't realize the water in the river was rising because they were running and they weren't watching the sides of the canyon, only what was in front of them. The wind picked up behind them. It came in thrusts rather than in a consistent breath.

A peregrine falcon shot up the canyon wall and rose above the edge and disappeared. It made Roy think that maybe they could find a route out, up the slick-rock, and wait on the lip of wall until the storm abated. But the wall hung over them like a cornice of snow, shaped as if it was a giant red wave curling over them. Where the light before had brought out the canyon's forms and patterns, it was as if they were now in a dark, gray tunnel.

Roy followed the bulge of Eric's pack, watched it lift and drop with each of his steps. He stopped, turned around and faced the wind head on. It strengthened in long gusts and then a pause and then repeated the pattern. The weight of rain was in his clothes. His shivering had turned to a hard, uncontrollable shaking.

Roy looked back. Eric hadn't heard him stop and was a good twenty yards away. He yelled at him. The noisy roll of thunder had increased tenfold, the water rushed at his feet, and the chaos of rain raised the level of sound to require shouting at that distance.

Eric saw Roy standing, facing upriver. He looked up. The storm clouds had lowered and sealed off the canyon from above. Did he know they were in trouble, that it was almost hopeless? Was he thinking about how he might save them, or did he want to let it go?

He shouted over the rising noise. "I'm in the desert now and I've got my gun!" He said as if God were right in front of him. He raised his imaginary gun to his temple. He squeezed his eyes shut. "Mother!" He shouted against the storm. "Am I worth saving?" He waited, his eyes were like bright bowls, but wild, "I'm sorry," he said and pulled the trigger.

Roy could barely make out the words, but could see his panic until Eric stopped, and a calm came over him as he stood against the oncoming river. Roy pushed against the swirling water now at his thighs and came up next to him.

"Tell my parents I'm sorry." Eric took him by the shoulders. "Tell Samantha what happened, everything. Make her know me."

Roy was scared now. "Your talking nonsense. Let's think about this."

Eric brought his mouth up to Roy's ear. "Tell Donna and Amanda, too. They should know. Everyone should know."

"Maybe we should let the river take us down. We'll take our packs off and float with the current."

"You'll get broken up over the rocks," Eric said. He moved out into the current, away from Roy, "Tell everyone!"

"Do you know a way out of the canyon from here?" Roy shouted after him.

"It's down further where we stopped before to look at the waterfall."

"Think we can make it?"

Eric turned back. "I'm done," he said, "and I don't have the energy. You should try though." Now Roy was wild, but Eric might have been talking about nothing.

"Aren't you worried?" Roy shouted.

"No, not really." Eric said. Then he took Roy's hands and held them like he did when they first met years ago. "Your hands are freezing," he said, then added, "I was worried, but I'm not now. Either way, I'm not going to make it, but you go."

"How do you know? You don't know what's happening."

"It's just a feeling, Roy, that's all." Eric let him go, removed the shoulder straps of his daypack and let it drop in the water. They both watched as it was carried out of sight in seconds.

The water rose faster. The wind came in sharper gusts, insistent on toppling them over.

Roy looked up and down the canyon. Both ends were enveloped in darkness. Thunder broke through its distance, now overhead, deafening and chilling. In flashes of lightning white, the slick-rock exploded in red rocket bursts flaring down canyon. The whole place was like some nighttime sound and light show. Both men stood in awe and watched for a moment before Roy realized that they were wasting time. He looked at Eric, and was startled to find him in a reverent repose taking in the sounds and sights of the world around him which was limited, at best, to him. Eric seemed to see beyond that and listened farther into the canyon for the echo of something he couldn't hear.

Eric turned towards Roy, "You'd better go, it's okay." He brought him close. "I love you very much. You should know that. And I know you love me. That's enough isn't it?" Roy nodded. "Now go, and see if you can make it out of here. Don't fight me to stay."

Roy forgot about the cold. Now he understood and began to cry. He was there in Eric's embrace then shook himself out of it. Some instinct for survival was still in him so he turned away from Eric. He moved to the edge of the river next to the canyon wall where the water was shallow, easier to run through.

The wind shifted hard, a biting extended thrust that carried the rain sideways. It peppered his back like pellets propelled by gunpowder.

The water swept past him, was muddier, the silt having turned it from clear blue to dull brown. He turned to see Eric angling himself towards the center of the river before going around a bend in the canyon. The water now was up above his waist. Eric's bright red jacket contrasted sharply against the dark.

Like before, Eric had gone off alone, separated himself from Roy who could now only watch as he extended his arms and held them out as if to embrace what came. He lifted his face to the rain and waited to be taken up.

All the world, all the sounds of earth, the final sigh of it, could be felt in how he held himself. This made Roy want to join him. He started back for Eric, tried to shout above the deafening thunder and the river which grew angrier, roiling loudly around his body, trying to take him with it. But he turned towards the cliff, started scrambling up, holding on to what little there was of limbs and outcroppings of stable rock. His arms ached. The rain beat down on his face making him blink it away. Under his feet, sandstone gave way and fell into the water below. With a final heave, Roy pulled himself up and over the ledge, falling flat on the plains muddy red surface. He turned and looked down to find Eric.

The flood came quickly. The river sucked away as if being gathered. Inside the canyon, a roar rose up like an arena full of spectators. The cliffs broke apart small avalanches of rock and sand. Lightning smacked down just above the cliffs electrifying the air. Water, a great wave of it, came around the bend in front of Eric and took him up into its full belly and crushed him inside its weight. Roy gathered himself up, up over the edge, a heaving mass, limbs stabbing over the ledge. He turned to see Eric one last time, a flash of red, a streak of blood piercing the mud of all the earth torn away by the force of water. But Roy turned and pulled himself up and ran away from the rise of rock, and kept on running, away from the blackness.

Epilogue

It was hours before the helicopters arrived so that the damage could be seen from overhead. As the pilot made his way up the canyon, he could see the Park entrance buildings ripped from their footings and lying sideways in the river. Cars were upended and strewn about its bed. Camping debris littered the tops of toppled trees that were stripped of their remaining leaves by the water's force. Parts of the road were washed away as was the bridge that crossed over the Virgin River with a southwest view towards Arizona.

The park was cleared of people except for those coming down from the top of Angel's Landing and other high trails that they'd been on. Remarkably, the rangers had gotten the small bunches of tourists who'd remained in the valley to high ground around the park. A few had been swept away, rescued, and accounted for by friends, in-laws and partners towards late afternoon.

It was only until after someone remembered passing two young men in the Narrows, who were heading upriver, that a search was begun.

They found the Blazer twisted around a tree, its front windowshield popped out and in pieces on the desert floor. The last of the sun glinted off them as if they were diamonds thrown in the sand. Search and rescue teams combed the truck checking for clues as to who owned it. They found the registration and the wallets for both of the men locked in the glove compartment.

Just before night fell, a pilot noticed a man lying at the lip of the canyon. He swooped in over him for a closer view and called for help. A couple of hours later Roy was airlifted to a hospital in St. George. He wouldn't say a word.

During the next few days, news people arrived from all over the West and some from the East. Roy's father came in from Los Angeles. Eric's family drove down from Salina and Salt Lake. A few friends came up from Las Vegas. The news people badgered them for interviews and any bit of information or insight they could give as to why the boys were up in the canyon on a day such as it was.

Each of them offered up their stories because the central force that bound them together now was gone, and they were alone in the world despite that some had wives, husbands or lovers waiting for their return.

Dusk came and the sky cleared leaving the stars to light one by one. Each of them knew that it would be a long time before they'd be able to go home.

My Kid in Footlights

I was standing at the back of the auditorium watching the chaos of color and kids readying themselves and each other for their play of *The Walrus and the Carpenter*. There was Nathan, a four-foot pirate, costume a little large, handed down, I heard, from another parent, flailing his arms around trying to get them in his brown vest. Monica was wailing because the head of the walrus, part foam rubber, nylon and gray paint, was choking her. She was the tallest – towering at nearly four foot five – besting by a few inches the tallest boy. The stars of the show were chosen according to height by Mrs. Wilson, the same as every year, so that all the other children, when clustered around The Walrus - and the Carpenter - could be seen by every parent; even the tardy ones who were forced to stand in back.

My wife, Susan, had the foresight to send our daughter along with Monica and her mother so she'd be on time. We are those perpetually late arrivers at events, parties, work, despite our best efforts. Plus, Monica's mother had a van, and our daughter Lily is playing an oyster. The chicken wire and scalloped foam contraption, covered in shiny pink fabric and held together by white glue, did not fit in either one of our cars. We had been looking, until recently, for a wagon or van.

I had come from work and called Susan on the way to let her know that I'd be there to help Lily with her costume. We communicated by cell phone now and the feeling was just as disembodied as if we were in person. It has been a week since I told her I was moving in with Steve which I let slip after a bottle of wine, two very dry martinis and a meal so heavy in carbohydrates my heart thumped wildly all night.

Driving home that evening from Steve's with his voice ringing in my ear, "It's now or never, Sam," I had that Beam Me Up transporter feeling of getting from one place to another without remembering the journey. While we lay together in Steve's bed, he rolled into me and whispered those words and then rolled away and left for the bathroom. I had put off the sheer terror of facing facts with Susan, who, I thought at the time, didn't have a clue, which made his ultimatum a difficult, unwieldy thing.

This past week has been about broken up cell phone negotiations with both Steve and Susan, worrying about my daughter, sleeping uncomfortably on the couch and sneaking in to our bed early in the morning so that when Lily came wandering in she'd see our marriage intact and provide that imaginary space between my wife and I, as if we'd drawn a pencil-thin line down the middle of the sheets – as if we were, like Lily, in third grade.

Lily ran toward me dragging the fragile oyster shell behind her. She was crying.

"What's the matter, hon?" I took the shell from her and laid it across the hard plastic theater seats.

"Mom didn't remember my tights!" Sure enough, Lily stood flat-footed before me in just the pink underpants without the pink leggings.

Escalating the problem I unwisely said, "Are you sure it was Mom and not you?"

"I need my tights!" Lily cried harder.

I put my hand on her shoulder. Other parents were turning around. I went for my cell phone. "Here, let's call her." At that prospect, Lily quieted. I dialed and put the phone to her ear. I heard Susan's phone ringing through mine. When it stopped, Lily waited a moment and then in a rush of words explained how she had left her tights, and how she needed them, and how rehearsal was just about to start for the group scene at the end and how Mrs. Wilson would be upset if she didn't have her whole costume.

"Here, let me talk to your mother." Lily turned to see if the other kids were gathering on stage. "Hi."

"Goddamnit," Susan said, "I'm almost there."

"I'll go get them. Lily will stay calmer with you."

"But you don't know where they are."

"Then tell me."

Lily slapped my leg. "Hurry. Tell Mommy to hurry!"

In a few minutes I was driving home. I'd given Lily over to another parent, Kristen Parker, whose boy was playing the Eldest Oyster, as if there were a hierarchy of oysters. As I was pulling out the school parking lot behind the auditorium, I saw Susan's blue Honda pull in the lot on the other side.

As I entered the house, the sun angled its way through the doors beveled, leaded glass, and struck the wood floor. I worked my way down the hall with the single purpose of finding Lily's pink leggings. But first, a beer to dull the sharp pain at the back of my neck; tension had worked its way through the knotted tangle of muscle. I turned towards the kitchen and saw the whole house before me – a giant ship of a room, hardly used, at its center.

The furniture was good: a notch above department store, but just below custom. The light was sufficient. Recently installed French doors, and an arbor to diffuse the light, gave the whole room a frosty snow-globe effect.

We'd had Lily late. We tried for years, spent thousands of dollars on fertility tests, drugs and procedures. We called her our Million Dollar girl. We'd had time to rid ourselves of the college collection and combine our separate tastes into décor that was somehow unified. Our house was more settled than those of other couples with kids the same age with their chaotic mishmashes of hand-me-downs and garage sales. The extra years of trying made all the difference.

We re-modeled everything just to take our minds off our failures. Instead of baby name books, it was *This Old House* or *Metropolitan Home* for me, and the Home Depot weekly circular for Susan. She'd bring home paint chips and tile samples and line them up for inspection on the kitchen counter. They'd be there for the week until she gathered more. I think she waited for me to say something, but I tried to keep myself casually indifferent thinking that those were decisions she wanted to make. Finally, after one of our Friday night dates we came home and she paused in the kitchen, snapped on the light, went to the refrigerator for ice cream and asked, "So, Sam, which combination?"

I gathered the bowls and spoons, "The gray slate colored tile and the blue."

"You think?"

"One scoop or two?"

"What day is this?" She went to the counting calendar and if it was past day ten in her cycle she cut her ice cream intake by half. I still don't know why. I really don't think it violated the reproductive cycle, but she always was careful about gaining weight when she couldn't exercise. It was easy enough to track. She numbered the days.

"Eight," I said, digging out the ice cream. "Two scoops then."

"Simple pleasures." She handed me the mint chip, the Haagen Daz, because at that time we still splurged and spent the big money where it counted. I became miserly when the medical bills and secret hotel charges started piling up.

I suppose I could lay the blame for our current predicament squarely at her feet. After all, *she* called him. I had nothing to do with it. Steve showed up one day to bring our electrical nightmares up to code. He wore blue jeans, a beige t-shirt with his company logo stretched over the pocket. They fit well.

Susan and I conceived, we birthed, we nurtured our little baby for three cycles of seasons.

Then our hybrid of knob and tube and the work Steve did years before simply couldn't withstand the three of us. So there he was, same exact uniform, on a Saturday with Susan and Lily at tumbling class and me working in the front yard.

When he came out of the truck deception followed him. For the next three years we had sex at his house where the lighting was excellent and dim, in hotels where it was harsh or dark, or in the cab of his truck late at night in shadowy places.

For the first time, I felt inadequate and liked it. I lost my grip on the rake, clumsily stooping to pick it up and return to the task of the leaves when Steve came around from the driver's side, clipboard in hand, ready to make assessments as he did every Saturday morning. He only worked half-days on the weekend and put it aside to bid on new jobs.

I remembered Steve. I saw him only a few times when he worked during the week that last time when Susan was home thinking of other projects to accomplish, nursing a tender belly. I remembered the full flush of him: his compact frame, the thick fingers, thinning blond hair, round open face, the shoulder-first walk where his body followed after it – not so much a swagger, but a statement – the eyes. No romantic notion there, for Susan's were just as deep a blue, and wise, and though I'm attracted to anyone's eyes first – it was the recognition.

Fall has always been my time for change. When most are settling in for the winter, I'm making plans. Plans for spring, plans for summer vacations, plans for how Susan and I would weather our barrenness. I go out and buy new sheets. I change from skivvies to boxers, white socks to dark. I get a new haircut, which lasts until the next one when I go back to the old look. Fall works on me like some hypnotist who has suggested in my sleep that every time the wind blows, or the buzzer on the dryer screams through the house, that I must change something. When Lily finally arrived, she became the beneficiary of this: new snuggly, new clothes, new shoes, whatever.

Of course, when Steve came to upgrade our electrical situation, it was fall.

I popped open the beer and surveyed the kitchen. It was the last thing we remodeled. Everything was almost new: the counters, cabinets, center island cook top, appliances, everything. Tonight it was cleared of all it had contained the night before when Susan built Lily's costume. Gone was the pearl pink fabric, the chicken wire, varying thicknesses of foam rubber, scissors, a hot glue gun, the paper pattern supplied by Mrs. Wilson.

For dinner, we'd ordered in. Susan ate in the kitchen, I in the great room – some inane TV show droned on. I called from the couch several times, "Do you need any help?"

"Just watch Lily," she said in syllables.

"She's playing in her room. I could help."

"No, I'll do it."

On through the night Susan worked. I went into our bedroom and fell asleep waking later to find her stretched out on the couch, blue TV light flickering across her. I stood there a moment taking her in. She'd removed her shoes and socks. My old white oxford gathered at her waist, then a strip of pale flesh, then blue jeans. Her thin hand lay across her belly, the other tucked under her breast as if holding herself close.

I found the remote on the floor in front of the couch, turned the TV off and went to the hall closet to retrieve a blanket. I shook it out. As it fell across her I took a last look at her body, its shape, its remote beauty before the blanket settled over her.

Susan had told me the leggings were in her room on the dresser. I was trying to assume that by saying 'her room' she'd meant Lily's room and not 'our' room which still contained our lives together; the pictures, our clothes – shirts of mine which she sometimes wore more than me – the small trinkets and knick knacks bought in Mexico, Hawaii and the European trek we'd made as part of our honeymoon.

There was the wooden Mayan fertility sculpture bought on our last trip to Cancun. Susan held it to her belly and closed her eyes after each insemination, where she felt nearly violated, and I felt silly handing over my semen in a cup to a nurse who treated it as just another sample by placing a lid on it, writing my name, and efficiently taking it down the hall to my waiting wife while I adjusted my pants, tucked in my shirt and waited in the hallway for the end of Susan's procedure. And what had once been an act of love had become a *procedure* and I was removed from it, had even thought of it in terms of a condition we had – an illness, a spent hip needing repair, a broken bone.

After we'd finally conceived, our lovemaking was different though we never addressed it. It became more clinical; as if we were still following instructions from the countless guides we'd read. I tried to get back to that space in my head where I had gone before, that little chamber that kept its door open for her, but it was as if some maze had constructed itself in front of the door. It would take me three years to find it again, but the chamber was of a different construction, and inside it contained Steve, and further inside it held the truth.

Having made the mistake of entering Lily's room, I understood that 'her' room had simply meant 'our' room. I went down the hall. Susan's clothes were on the floor, the bed was unmade, and the drapes were pulled against the late afternoon sun. I turned on the dresser lamp and there the pink tights were bunched like a bouquet, waiting to be snatched up, remembered.

I sat on the unmade bed and parlayed the rest of my beer into a moment of contemplation. I gazed across the room at all the things we'd collected; the armoire which contained the TV and a library of videos, ranging from Disney to home edited celebratory tapes. The home version of a Stairmaster in the corner had become a sort of valet with clothes hanging from it; an array of framed pictures - how obsolete they were becoming - dotted the bookshelf. How was it so different after so many years, and how was it that Steve's bedroom had become more like home, more a place of rest.

Can a room become a burden, a weight? Can love become *procedure*? I dreaded falling into bed at night, even when Lily had first crawled out of her crib, climbing precariously over the rails and making her way from her room to ours, finally standing at the foot of the bed looking at us, her big eyes questioning, and us untangling ourselves and looking down to see her head bobbing just above the comforter. I thought those moments would be magical, but I found them intrusive suddenly and what I'm feeling might be selfish, or might be necessary, but it may just be the thing that propelled me towards Steve.

The smell of a room too can change, what was sweet and right can addle you, can turn sour as old milk. I tried putting my finger on it, but there it was, in the towels, my clothes, *her* clothes. It was a pervasive thing, like cold in winter. And I can sit here and say that everything was different at Steve's – *his* towels, *his* clothes, and the way *he* smelled, but that wouldn't be right either. It seemed as if I carried this odor with me like a curse and, sifting through clothes, through belts and socks, pants and sweaters, throwing them on the bed, I wanted those smells back.

I went to the hall closet, pulled a duffel bag down and then back to the bedroom, to the dresser. I quickly packed my things. I noticed smells I loved returning and recognized them – leather, eucalyptus, saltwater.

The phone rang.

"Where are you?" Susan said.

"There was traffic."

"Why are you out of breath?"

My mind shuffled like a jukebox. "I ran from the car."

"Did you find them? We have a bit of time. Mrs. Wilson can't seem to get all the children together and they still have to rehearse once before the performance. Can you believe we're not the last to arrive?"

"I've got Lily's tights in my hand." In fact I was stuffing a couple of sweatshirts and t-shirts into the growing bag.

Susan seemed distracted as well. "See you in a few?"

"On my way." I said and snapped the phone closed.

I went into the bathroom to find my razor and the other things I hadn't duplicated at Steve's. Behind the vanity mirror were the yellow vials of pills left over from our reproductive trials. Pills to boost my semen, pills to boost her hormones, every conceivable thing. Why they all hadn't been tossed seemed calculated now, as if Susan were reminding me daily of the struggle.

I could have easily thrown them out myself, but I had simply passed them over during my morning routine. Twisting the bottles to read their labels, I thought of Lily and the day she came home from the hospital – a bundled packet of triumph over nature. The workings of science against what we couldn't do naturally; all these little pills perverting our chaotic internal fluids into reproductive order.

I'd watched Steve put in the small, white globes over the bathroom mirror, stretching his short frame to reach with his hand drill and secure their bases into place. He dropped one and it crashed spectacularly sending out sharp little fragments all over the floor and into the bedroom.

"Fuck!" he shouted and poked his head around the door to see if anyone was there. I was leaning against the dresser. "Oh, sorry."

"Don't mind me."

"I meant for the kid." He crunched through the glass and came into the bedroom.

"I'll go get the vacuum." I left him there amid the shattered glass, standing a little awkward in someone else's bedroom. I'd always thought how odd it must be to work in and around other people's private rooms and things.

We picked up the larger pieces and then I vacuumed the rest. We moved around each other like fish picking a piece here, there. I felt his heat. Streaks of sweat ran down his t-shirt. I touched him. He closed his hand around a tiny shard and when he opened it again it had drawn blood.

I shivered. We both looked at the tiny red point in his hand. He put his other on my shoulder and pulled me toward him. He kissed me. After an hour, the carpet was clothes-covered, Steve and I were heaped together, legs tucked, sweat-soaked, bodies forcing air. Lily was three then; I was thirty-six; Susan, thirty-four.

For the next three years Steve and I tangled together when we could, when

Susan took Lily to her parents, when I went out for errands. No time seemed to be good to make the split. Two of our parents died, Steve's sister broke her marriage and moved in with him for a time. Holidays were horrible: me wanting two things at once.

I snapped the bathroom light off. I picked up Lily's tights, the duffel bag and made my way out to the front foyer. I looked around. Am I good at anything other than leaving? I feel like a chicken-shit. I've failed at marriage, at loving my kid enough, at being able to fix things myself. What kind of man leaves his family?

Late afternoon became evening. People walked their dogs. Baby strollers were pushed. Mothers made dinners. Baseball practice was over. Soccer girls removed their shoes. Fathers pulled into their driveways and switched off their ignitions. The whole world darkens, but houses light up, are lit from within.

I was standing there while Susan waited, and Lily was waiting and Steve paced around his home the way he does, waiting. I switched the lights on in my old house and left.

I made it back to Lily's school between the rehearsal and performance. I helped her with the tights and wished her well. I couldn't look at her. I joined Susan in the back and we smiled at each other. It was the first time since last Saturday when I told her about Steve and she'd wondered aloud how come it took so long.

She mouthed, "Thank you," and I nodded my head. The theatre went black. The Walrus and the Carpenter were center stage. They began to tentatively recite the poem and all the parents laughed, video cameras rolled, flashbulbs sparked. I was overcome with love.

"I'm going to stay with Steve tonight."

"I thought you might."

"He said he'd fix anything in the house for free if it goes bad."

Susan snapped her fingers, "Just like that?"

"What?"

"I snap my fingers and he'll come running?"

"Susan, don't."

"Maybe I'll go home and rip out all the wiring." She hissed and stared straight ahead at the children gathering around the walrus. "Can he fix that?"

A woman in front turned and shushed us. The oysters were now about to be led astray. Lily was down in front near the footlights for she was the littlest, her pink tights too large and bunched at the knees. She was smiling because she had to, but I could tell she was upset because the pink oyster shell fabric had fallen away from the foam. Later she will complain that all the other kid's costumes were better, but now she is preparing to fall down, on cue, when the walrus reaches out its large, cardboard flipper and pretends to eat her.

Mrs. Wilson had fashioned footlights from coffee cans, painted their outsides black, put 60-watt bulbs inside so the light reflected warmly on stage. I wondered how she wired them underneath, whether they were all separate wires dangling down attached to a straight plug, or whether she'd taken the time to fasten them together along one wire, the electricity coursing through, lighting up everything that needed to be seen.

The Road to Alaska

This year, the snow had a diminishing effect on Rob.

He watched it everyday from his window, covering the houses and streets, the cars, and sometimes the telephone and electrical wires. He let his dog out a few times each day, stepping out long enough to feel the chill and scrape away the heavy white from the top step. By the time he was finished, the dog came back in and shook himself out over the wooden floor. Then he'd go back to the kitchen table, which was covered by a collection of travelogues, newspapers and magazine articles — every one of them about Alaska.

When he sat down to eat he didn't bother to move them out of the way. Instead, he put his bowl of soup over Sitka or Juneau, read about the hard climbs up Mt. McKinley, about the inland waterways through the vast chunks of land where natives hunted wildlife, or the histories of fishing villages along the Aleutian Islands that ran like a surprised eyebrow up over the Gulf.

At night, he dreamt about the land, mulled it over in his thoughts. He woke in the earliest hours and went back to the breakfast room, switched on the gilded chandelier over the table and peered down at Alaska, as if he were God trying to imagine and manipulate the mountains to angle up across the vast expanse of land separating rivers and plains, the cold breaks of ice and rivers. He'd be endlessly fascinated, wishing he could see it first hand.

Rob's father had promised to take him there, but he has taken his mother and brother before him, so that now the excitement of going with his father had abandoned him. He'd decided to go himself. In the spring, with the snowmelt, he'd pack his bag and head out to Alaska alone.

Maybe Rob shouldn't have mentioned to his father that he was gay. He'd outlined that fact in a letter he sent. If he'd fleshed out what was hastily written, he probably wouldn't have gotten a call from his father telling him he'd be flying in that weekend for a short visit.

A year passed since Rob had seen his parents, and exactly three since he'd had a lover. In the middle of the second year, he'd gone out and gotten himself a dog for company. But the shepherd could only do so much and he'd started looking for another lover. He asked men on dates, dinner at The Iguana Cafe, a drive up to the ski resorts for a walk around, or he made dinner at home. Mostly they'd end up at the local bar, sneaking glances at other men. It was going to be easy to keep the weekend for his father clear.

He planned gambling in Wendover, maybe take him out to the new restaurant South of the Temple where the Mormon's never dared poke their head; the restaurant was liberal about their liquor. There was the drive out to the deserts where the snow stuck to the ground for only a moment. He could also plan nothing and let the weekend take its course.

The morning of his father's arrival, he took each of the maps, folded and banded them together, then stuck them neatly in a drawer where he knew his father wouldn't go. He returned the books to the library, paid the overdue fines, but not before writing their names down so he could check them out again the following Monday. He set up a block of wood in the center of the breakfast table and placed a fired, green bowl on top of it.

He shoveled snow from the walkway, cleared a path from the street to the front door where he'd let his father out at the curb. Rob wanted to do this to give him a clear view of the house he'd bought the year before. From the street one could take in the sloping, gabled roof, the clean, white exterior and the newly painted shutters that framed the windows. As he walked up the steps, his father could turn around and inspect the neighborhood and he'd see that his son had bought in a good one.

He'd hide from his father that just up the street was a man who'd been accused of molesting a little girl, that the Andrews three doors down sometimes came shouting at each other into the driveway as the wife ran to the car and sped off down the street, sometimes skidding across the new snowfall like some drunkard navigating a sidewalk.

There'd be no mention of the woman that came to the house across the street where the husband spent the day at home while his wife left each morning for work and came home each evening at exactly the same time.

Finally, he'd neglect to tell his father about the stake bishop next door, who'd drop by at odd hours and ask Rob questions that gave him the indication that the bishop envied Rob's life, the way he'd catch the bishop watching from he and his wife's bedroom window as the various men left from his house. The Bishop never specifically said anything, but he'd smile at him and watch as that night's lover negotiated the frozen driveway down to his car.

There were other things, and on that early Saturday morning, during the drive out of Salt Lake towards the airport, past the fields of honey-colored grass sticking up out of the islands of snow, Rob became a little panicked. He wanted to cling to the last few moments of being alone before the weekend, but the high wind and swirling highway snow kept his attention to the road.

The last time he was on this particular highway, a golden eagle was hunched over a road kill, spiking it with its muscular neck. Rob saw its talons and beak pulling up the strands of flesh before he realized what it was as he sped past. He recalled the greatness of its size and marveled that he hadn't spooked the eagle. He narrowly missed a cement guard, so Rob put his mind to the curve into the airport expressway that led him towards the curb where he could quickly pick up his father.

As he rounded into the arrival area, he saw him standing there working his umbrella open against the falling snow. His father wore a plain colored overcoat, the kind you see in cop shows, with the vacant fronts, the double rows of buttons traveling up both sides of fat bellies. But his father was thin, he could see that; he'd lost weight since the last time he saw him.

Rob honked his horn lightly and his father turned toward him and forgot about the umbrella, never having figured the way to open it. Rob assumed his mother must have handed it to him before his father left her for the weekend.

And though the weather outside could be measured in the high thirties, Rob's face grew slack and clammy and his palms slipped on the hard plastic steering wheel. When he reached over to push the passenger door open, he felt a trickle of sweat itch down the middle of his chest as his shirt loosened. He almost forgot to get out to put his father's bags in the trunk. When he did he shook his legs so they'd work properly.

When they met at the trunk, Rob looked at his father who, in turn, gazed just over Rob's shoulder, past the terminal towards the high range of mountains in the distance. Rob didn't know what to say; he came to realize in the last few years that there was no history between them, nothing to conjure up conversation. He offered his hand.

"Hi, Dad," he said, "Glad you could make it out." Rob noticed the bags under his father's eyes, how heavy they'd become. He saw how the skin on his face had loosened and the lines of his neck deepened. His Dad's handshake went limp before Rob wanted it to, so Rob squeezed again and his father's energy reappeared slightly.

"You seem a bit tired," he said.

"I got up early to catch the plane, well, I was actually already up. Your mother gets out of bed so damn early every morning." Rob bent over and picked up the bag and swung it over the back end and squeezed it in over the contents of the trunk. Rob remembered that he'd decided to clean his trunk out before his father got there, but he'd forgotten.

"Let's get out of here. Climb in." They sped away from the curve a bit too carelessly for his father's comfort. Of course, he was used to the LA airport, the professional van drivers that abused the outside lane. Rob instinctually knew there'd be no one coming through, not this early on a Saturday after the ski season was over and spring hadn't really begun.

They didn't say a word on the way out of the airport, not until they reached the cashier at the end of the drive when they both went for their wallets to pay the toll. His father got to his wallet first, so Rob stopped and gripped the steering wheel as he braked to a stop at the booth.

"I've got it," said his father.

"That's fine." Rob took the one-dollar bill and stuck it out through the small opening at his window. He nodded to the attendant, then waited for the black and white arm to raise. As they approached the highway, they saw two ducks fly in and land at the pond landscaped into the center of the airport grounds.

"Pintails. They're heading North again," said his Dad, "heading up to Canada, I suspect."

"They're kind of early, but I've been noticing some of the geese coming back up the valley." With the two of them in the car, the windows fogged. Rob switched on the noisy defroster, which buzzed all the way back into town.

Halfway in, his dad turned slightly in his seat towards his son. There was a long moment. Rob looked at him.

"You okay?"

"I was just thinking."

"About?"

"What would you say about driving up to the Grand Tetons." His dad sort of laughed and turned back in his seat.

"You're kidding, right?" Rob glanced over and met his father's eyes.

"No, I'm not."

"I don't have my stuff. And I only have about ten bucks on me." Rob felt a sort of odd sensation come up his spine like a chill, but he kept it down and willed it away.

"I'll buy you what you need." His dad leaned over and looked at the car's gauges. "We need gas, so why don't you pull off and fill up the tank."

"You're serious about this, aren't you?" Rob looked down at the instrument panel and tried to remember the last time he changed his oil.

His father bent his head down and looked at his hands, "Yeah, I guess so."

The drive up into the flats above the canyon out of the valley was quiet; through Coalville and around the small lakes, the condensation in the car froze in the corners of the windows. The heater chugged out warm air into the cabin, and Rob put his hands against the vents to warm his fingers. His father offered him his gloves that he'd pulled out of his suitcase, but Rob refused them.

His father sat with his face towards his window most of the time looking out at the snow. Once they passed Coalville the landscape didn't much change save for the ponds. When they passed those he'd remark every time that it was still too early for the birds up here, that maybe their flyway only ran through the Salt Lake valley. Rob told him about the geese, pintail and mallard ducks, the small goslings and ducklings he'd seen there in the spring and summer.

"I would imagine they'd venture up here later, I guess. Maybe we should have waited," his father said.

"We could turn back." Rob suggested. He'd secretly been holding out for a reason to turn around and forget the whole thing, maybe drop him back at the airport for an earlier flight back to Los Angeles.

"No. Can't do that." His father spread his hand around his thigh and squeezed it to get the blood flow moving again.

"What? Why not?"

"Just can't, that's why." His Dad brought his head up and looked squarely at Rob, looked hard at him so that he finally had to turn back to the highway when he felt a wheel dip off into the shoulder.

Rob felt himself tighten - and surprisingly a feeling of worry for his father welled up inside of him - so that down into the pit of his stomach he sensed a deep dissatisfaction within his Dad. But he'd gotten used to letting any feelings for his father fall from him.

"We'll pull off in a bit and grab us a couple of beers," Rob slapped the dashboard to break the mood, "How about that?"

"Sounds good. I can use a stretch." His Dad fiddled with the radio dials. "I suppose all there is up here is country music."

"My radio doesn't pick up much, but you can try." Rob's father sped through the static sometimes catching the hint of a song or a voice. Then he switched the radio off and pushed himself back into the bucket seat and followed the land with his eyes.

At the border of Utah and Wyoming, they left the road and pulled into Evanston, where twenty or thirty liquor stores were lined up, all of them beckoning. Some had drive-thru signs surrounded by small bulbs where only a few of them blinked; other stores had bright, neon circles advertising specials. Utahns went there to buy real beer and alcohol at rock-bottom prices. When Rob pulled into the parking space at the front of one of them, he had to laugh at the dilapidated stores that were built during the seventies to support the local oil boom, he wasn't used to seeing so much alcohol in one place.

"My God," he said, "an alcoholic's paradise." Rob stepped onto the plowed parking lot, shook his bad knee out. He watched his Dad get out of the car and test the ground before he fully emerged.

"I wore the wrong shoes." He examined his feet as he stood up, then kicked the soles of his loafers into the scraped ice over the pavement. "I should never have let your mother tell me to wear these shoes. She insisted though and the thing is is that I know what kind of shoes I should have worn. I'm not stupid, you know."

"We'll get some boots for you in Jackson," Rob said, somewhat alarmed. "Just be careful 'til we get there." Rob went into the store followed by his ill-tempered father. They picked out beers and Rob offered up his last ten dollars to the man at the cash register who was heavy and leaned perilously to the left. When he moved Rob noticed that his left leg was small and bent.

"Save it," his father said holding out a five to the cashier.

"If it were me, mister, I'd let him pay for it," the cashier smiled at the father.

"You think so?"

"If he's offering. Hell, I wish my boy would do that sometimes." Rob caught the cashier glancing his way and handed the man his ten. He took it and made change. "Possibility, mister. You made it possible for him to buy you that beer." Rob took the change and stuffed it back into his pocket and flicked the top on the beer can.

"I suppose I did," said the father smiling.

"Damn straight you did," said the cashier.

"Let's go." Rob grabbed his beer and headed for the door.

Once in the car, Rob drank fast. He crumpled up the can in his strong grip and let it fall to the floor. His father lowered himself into the car butt-first, stomped the hard soles of his shoes on the ground, realized that it didn't do any good, and finally swung his legs in.

"It doesn't matter about the snow," Rob said.

"I'm not worried about the snow, it's my toes I'm worried about. I can feel the snow melt going after them."

"Stick 'em up against the heater then."

"Goddamn these shoes."

158

"Are you sure you still want to go all the way to Jackson?"

"You don't want to go?" his father asked.

"It doesn't matter to me. I was hoping to show you my house. You haven't seen it yet."

"We'll see it on the way back." Rob's dad took a small sip from the beer. "My mouth is dry. It's dry air up here, isn't it?"

"Not a speck of moisture." Rob started the car, eased it into gear and backed out onto the main street. His father fidgeted in the seat, shuddered the cold out of his body and settled back in.

Rob noticed how his father had begun picking up the movements of old men. He cocked his head forward to listen, felt parts of his body to see if there was still play left in the muscles, rubbed his eyes and asked questions about road signs after they passed them. His father was still young enough. On his last birthday, Rob called home to learn that he'd taken off for the day, made some excuse to his mother about letting the day just pass by without event.

Back into the drive, Rob relaxed, put an elbow up on the rest between the seats and felt his father's arm there and leaned into it a little. He felt a slow wave of warmth come over him, like a filament heater sparking to life. His eyes caught the glittering snow as the sun began angling down into afternoon.

Heat. His father needed that, he could feel it: something in his mind began to form in the shape of his mother and he believed she was part of it. Why else, in the face of the letter's news, would he keep his elbow so firmly against his?

Farther down the road his father suddenly said, "We Waverly men never live past seventy," he paused, "that about gives me a little over ten years." This made Rob sit up, take stock of the highway again. He'd sort of dozed off, not like in sleep, but that curious plane he drifted into when his mind began turning, shutting out the concrete things that were in the present. In this state, he went into the past. When he did this he sunk into a depression that worked itself through his body. Sometimes he became physically despondent, as if his limbs were weighted down. Most of the time he couldn't explain it.

"What do you mean?" Rob asked.

"Well, let's see. Not one of the men in our family has made it to seventy. Uncle Stephan came within a blink of seventy, but he collapsed one day out of sheer exhaustion. Your Uncle only got to sixty-two. My father, well you know what happened to him."

"Why are you bringing this up?"

"Because it needs to be said." His father took out a pack of gum, unfolded a pink, flat stick from its wrapper, then placed it on his tongue as if to melt it.

"I want to do a lot of traveling before I'm sixty-five. That way I won't be

159

hedging my bets on making it to seventy."

"Jesus, Dad."

"You're too young to think about things like this and you probably shouldn't."

"I think about it all the time," Rob said. And that, Rob thought, was the essence of the wide gulf he'd created between them. So he waited for a question from his father, something that would prove his ignorance, but his father surprised him.

"Yes," he said, "I suppose you do." Rob's dad slowly folded the gum wrapper in a tiny square and placed it back into the larger packet. Then the noise of the road filled the cabin again and both of them drifted back into their own thoughts.

For the remainder of the drive up into the Teton Valley, their conversation rose and fell in timid fits and starts. Neither one of them ventured past the safe territory of an almost pre-determined set of topics; work, family, travel. When they began to move out of those shallow waters, the conversation dried up as if it was sucked outside the car and left behind. And when they rounded the initial bend into the valley along the highway, the last of the topics fell away and the Grand Tetons rose up like glacial cathedral towers.

Rob and his father pulled into the small turnout the plows had made at the viewpoint that in spring and summer is rimmed with a ring of golden flax. Now, however, the snow banded the flat valley to the base of the Tetons. The eye followed the white expanse up and into the air as the snow blew off the high peaks and formed temporary rainbows when the light pierced the crystals at a perfect angle.

Rob and his father got out of the car, walked towards the mountains a few steps and just stood there and looked. There was no sound but the hissing of a light wind. They could see movement out past the Snake River that wound its way down the middle of the valley. Elk moved leisurely across the plain, glad for the warmth of the sun. It seemed as if they were heading back up into the cauls between the rocky towers towards the safety of the park.

Another car pulled violently into the turnout shattering the silence. Rob and his Dad turned to look and watched as the car skidded wildly into a snow bank that was hard and crusty, having been heated up and frozen several times over during the course of the winter. The bending and crunching of the fender was heightened by the quiet.

Rob said, "Jesus. I wonder if he's drunk." He saw the man slam his hands into the steering wheel and blindly reach for the indoor handle of the car. The woman next to him reached out and grabbed him as the man came tumbling out of the driver's side and slipped on the ice. Rob started towards him, but his father pulled him back and held on to his coat.

His father said, "Don't," then reached up, rested his hand on Rob's shoulder and turned him back towards the view of the mountains.

The man cussed and slammed his door and loped away from the car.

From the corner of his eye Rob could see he was a big man, legs and rear-end bigger than the rest of his body. As the man ran out into the snowfield he threw his arms into the air, then shook them like he was vigorously polishing something.

The woman came into view and tugged on the back of his jacket. He kept moving into the white expanse as she struggled into a coat and gloves.

"Come back to the car," she said. "Come back. It's so cold."

"I'm not going any farther," the man shouted, "I can't do it. I took out four days and you do this. You bring me down, Karen. You just up and bring me down.... tearing at me and tearing at me till I got nothing to say. So you just let me out here. Take the car, Karen." The man looked back to the car, it was still running, the tailpipe twisting the engine smoke into the air. "Take it. I'll find my own way back."

Rob's father moved his hand from Rob's shoulder and held onto his elbow. Rob could feel his grip grow stronger, but he just let it. The couple mesmerized his father and Rob saw that he had no intention of leaving so Rob didn't suggest it.

"You can't," the woman said, "you can't do that."

The man and woman moved farther into the field. Their shouts rang like shrill bells out over the stillness. It was strange how the air changed the cadence of their voices, how it bent them over the waves of the vast open space. They continued shouting at each other for ten minutes. The man ripped branches from the low bushes then threw them to the ground. He shook his legs of snow every so often after he sunk into some of the deeper pockets. They alternated moving towards each other then moving away, like two upturned magnets being forced together. Rob wondered if they'd noticed his father and he standing, watching; he wondered if they cared or not.

"I can't believe they're still out there and they're shouting at each other like that. I mean look where we are!" His father still had his hand on his arm and now Rob could feel the grip trembling slightly. He snuck a look at his father and saw that he was crying. "Dad, what's wrong?"

"At least they're in love," he said. Then he wiped across his face with the crook of his arm, looked at his son, and shifted his eyes sideways over Rob's shoulder. "I thought I was in love once with your mother. I was wrong."

"What are you saying, Dad?" Rob hated his father's habit of looking past him. "Look at me," he said.

"We never got to the point of feeling like those two." Then his father took his hand away from his son, stared straight into Rob's eyes unblinking, his own rounded by a soft swelling of red, and began to tell him the whole sad story of his marriage to Rob's mother. During the course of it, Rob had a thought that no one could really know their parent's relationship, the complexities, the hurt and pain they inflict on each other, one could only rely on what they saw, and in his father's case he saw the rueful arc of a realization come too late.

After he finished talking, his father pulled Rob's letter out of his jacket pocket, held it up, his hand shaking and white from the cold. "I hope you find someone to love Rob. I really do." Then he handed the single piece of paper back to Rob whose body went rigid; as if he'd suddenly taken the cold of the afternoon air into his lungs and held it there.

His father walked away from him and headed to the car. Remembering the couple, he turned and looked back and saw them. They'd come together finally. The man rested on an exposed rock while the woman stood between his legs wrapped in his arms. Their car was still idling.

Rob came up to him and said, "Let's go home."

"Would you mind if I stayed a couple of extra days?"

"Stay as long as you want," Rob said, as he opened the passenger door and watched his father slide into the cold seat. He went around the back of the car to his side and stopped to throw the ball of paper into the air out towards the mountains. It didn't go very far, but the light wind picked it up enough so that it dipped over a snowdrift and disappeared.

Later in the car, speeding out of the Teton valley and heading back, Rob looked at his father sitting there. He wondered how he'd gotten so small. Then, wanting to make him as large as he remembered him, Rob turned and said, "Tell me about Alaska, Dad."

"What do you want to know?"

"Everything."

Follow Me Through

I've watched the chaotic lives of children, bristled at their loud screams in movie theaters, and heard the ravings and crying of the downstairs neighbor kid - those shrill, explosive outpourings of need and anger. I've even buried my head under a pillow listening to the woman next door slamming her way through the kitchen making formula for her baby. So why, then, was there a small baby sitting next to me in my car, lifted quietly and easily from a department store in the middle of a gigantic mall, surrounded by swirls of traffic and rushing people making their way home for Christmas Eve?

He sat there, wide-eyed, not realizing his fate, watching me with those brown eyes, his hair swirled like shaved chocolate on fancy cakes; his legs and arms pushing and pulling in the air, automatically moving against what came, which was nothing but the blue crushed velour of the bucket seat I'd strapped him into.

I pulled out into the rush of red and white lights, made a mad dash into the oncoming night, cars moving with a purpose, the blinking, blinking, blinking of turn signals and streetlights and the odd strand of Christmas bulbs. He gurgled and yipped like a puppy, the curious sounds coming from his mouth in a quick barrage of self-involved movements. I put my hand on his leg to calm him down.

I must confess. It had been easier than I thought. I sat for two hours outside of the department store, in the open circular expanse of the indoor mall, watching people ascend and descend on escalators, fight their way around slow-walking shoppers, or stop momentarily to take bites out of ice cream cones that were sold next to the wide opening of the store where I committed the crime.

I saw him coming in a stroller, being pushed by his mother. She was momentarily crushed as an oncoming group of people bottlenecked their way down a ramp as she navigated herself and the stroller the opposite way. When she emerged, she stopped and adjusted the packages draped over both arms and absentmindedly let the stroller drift away from her a little.

I stood up, brushed my hair away from my eyes, and moved in behind her as she worked her way into the store's wide mouth. In two minutes she lost herself among the fragrances, powders and lipsticks. Saleswomen pushed sample bottles toward her. You could almost hear the whish! of a thousand perfume bottles going off at once.

When the mother turned away and moved down the length of the brightly lit counter, I lifted the small baby out of the stroller and carried him quickly away.

Coming into my apartment, everything seemed to slow down again, the air settled and I was able to breathe for the first time in a long, long while. I sat the baby down on the living room floor that I'd vacuumed only hours earlier. I placed stuffed animals, the small bears I'd been given as presents, around him. I stared at the baby and guessed him to be about nine months. I went and turned the heat up in the apartment. The baby played, chewed on the small arms and legs of the beige animals as I went to heat water. I plugged in the Christmas tree lights. The sparkling tinsel came to life as colors reflected from it. I took my jacket off and hung it up in the closet off the hall leading into the bedroom. I switched on lights and turned on Christmas carols.

Paul had known all the words to them, but he was gone now. I took his blanket off the bed, the one that had kept him warm when he was sick. I'd since gotten it laundered and shook it out into the air by the baby. He crawled across it and brought it over his head. I watched him from the kitchen as I put a bottle in the warm water.

In the supermarket earlier, I collected various jars and boxes of formula and baby food. There were crushed peas, tapioca pudding and creamed carrots. I chose boxes of specially formulated oatmeal, sterilized packages of formula envelopes, an assortment of juices and protein powders. I spent over an hour in the market, the checker looked at me and smiled, "New baby?"

"Yes," I said, "new, very new."

"Isn't that nice. I hope your wife is doing okay."

I paused, looked at her, "Oh yes, fine, just fine."

"Do you have a name yet?"

"I believe I'll call him Paul."

"That's a nice name." She ran the items over the red-infrared beams with her fat hands. I scratched my forehead then left my fingers there. "It's a family name."

Cheerfully the checker looked at me and smiled, "That's nice. That'll be forty-two thirty-seven." I handed her a fifty.

When I got home, I put the army of groceries on the counter and stepped back to survey the kitchen and decide where to put things.

I'd scrubbed the counter they sat on, taken steel wool and bleach to the grout between the tiles. I removed any of Paul's germs that may have lingered from his underwear and bandages that I washed in the kitchen sink every day for six months. I'd taken the orange plastic bottles of pills and thrown each of them in the trash, but not before reading each of the labels once more. I tried to remember at which point we'd been prescribed the particular drug, each horrifying one. I'd donated the plastic saline bags, the remaining bandages and tubing to the hospice where Paul would have gone had I let him.

I pulled the plastic bottle from the water, tested the formula against my arm. I bent down to give him the bottle. He looked up and smiled, grabbed at his food, needy. I straightened up and towered above him, his small hands working the bottle against his body capable as an otter.

He sucked at the nipple fervently. It was not unlike preparing the drugs for Paul to send through the permanent catheter affixed to his chest, the liquid dripping down from the saline bag and mixing as Paul sat and listened to me read from a newspaper or from a story I thought he'd like. His eyes finally disintegrated enough to shut out details like printed text or the stairs leading down to the street. He grabbed at the rail in the first few weeks and inched down. As his eyesight worsened he became more adept at descending, sometimes throwing a Norma Desmond pose or pretending to be Fred Astaire sending my heart to my throat every time he tried that one.

The baby emptied the bottle and I picked him up and bounced him against my shoulder around the apartment. His breathing was labored and scattered as he worked the bubble up from his body and onto the towel I draped just under his head. I pulled him away from me and held him up. "Done?" He just stared at me and bobbed his head from side to side. His hand came for my glasses and I jerked my head back. "No, no you don't."

I set him back down on the floor where his eyes rolled back and fluttered.

The heat from the apartment and the sedating formula were taking a toll on him. He started to whimper a bit so I picked him up again and took him from room to room trying to get him to sleep. We went into the second bedroom.

I flicked on the light. I said to the little boy, "This is Paul's room. This is where he died." I placed my hand softly over the baby's head while he struggled against sleep. "I've thrown everything out, though, so practically nothing's left to get to know him by. I just figured his sickness was like scarlet fever and everything had to be destroyed. I couldn't take the chance anyway." The baby's breathing slowed and he became damp and clammy against my breast and arm.

I sat on the edge of the hospital bed I'd rented for Paul under his insurance plan. I hadn't called to have it taken away, though now I couldn't afford the extra seventy-five dollars it would cost me each month. I'd stripped the sheets, threw them away and covered the stiff mattress with an old patterned blanket I'd kept from before we'd met.

I lowered the baby to the bed and went into the other room to get him a blanket. The heat from the wall furnace hadn't yet reached the bedroom. I'd kept a portable heater in the corner for Paul when he had night sweats. When there was no light in the room, the burning filament cast a glow over the stiff sheets. As he wasted away I could only see how the red glow lowered down the wall like a sunset as his shape disappeared.

I sat back down, rolled the baby over on his stomach and covered him up. I turned to the darkness of the room, folded my hands into my lap and looked around the sparsely furnished space. The terrible, sad thing was I couldn't see Paul anymore, I'd cleaned up after him so well.

His parents hated the fact that we were lovers. His mother brushed me off as though I were a speck of dust landed on the blackest of her satin dresses she wore for almost every occasion. She sent home pictures of her and Paul, Paul and grandmother, Paul and father, combinations of other family and Paul, which he'd frame, then put them in his own groupings. Even after all the years we were together, I was absent from every photograph. But Paul would go to her dinner parties, then come home light, but exhausted, whistling some tune his mother had played on her black piano, a shrine to her failed music career. Paul played for the symphony until he lost precision in his arms and fingers after a particularly harsh attack by our disease to his nervous system.

And I say *our* disease because we reveled in it - each new medical discovery, herbal treatment, vitamin therapy or new way to induce betacarotin into our systems, without having to actually drink straight carrot juice. We tacked clippings up on our daily bulletin board from newspapers, magazines, medical journals and hastily written homemade prescriptions from friends throughout the Avenues and up through Capitol Hill. For a time it seemed like it all might work, but reality plays a nasty trick on the body and Paul would lie awake at night and tell me he could actually feel the virus working it's way through his body as dye through water.

In the face of his parents he opted to call me his friend to them as if there was nothing more between us than pasta and a movie Saturday nights. When he told them he was positive, they hated me even more. The worst part though was that they blamed me, which I understood, because Paul was negative before he met me and I had come up positive several months into our relationship.

When Paul began to get sick, I felt there was nothing I could do but be there, clean up after him. When our first doctor came in, saw Paul shaking to beat the band, he looked at me and asked, "How long have you been lovers?"

"We've been *partners* twelve years."

The doctor dropped his head for a moment, slipped on the rubber gloves. He looked at me then, "It's amazing how many people get offended at the word 'lover.'" He pressed a thumb on a spot near Paul's neck like you would a cantaloupe." I make no distinction, I guess. It's a matter of priorities. I expect lovers to get sick, not partners."

When Paul first announced he was getting sick, he stood in the doorway of our bedroom. He usually discovered things about his body in the morning, when he came out of the shower puffy and steamy to examine the pounds he'd gained or lost the day before. Paul came from the light into the dark next to my side of the bed.

"You see this?" He turned the inside of his thigh towards me, lifted up his balls. I pulled my head off of the pillow and looked. It was too dark.

"No, what?" Paul reached over and flicked on the bedlamp and pointed at a purplish spot on his leg. "It's starting." he said.

This was four years ago.

From then on, Paul's examinations became laborious and I was made to look at each developing lesion or loss of weight with the careful precision of a gem cutter. Each time I put my mouth to the spot and kissed it lightly. I stroked his leopard legs, arms and neck. When he shook from shingles I'd lay my naked body, still thick and fleshy through the middle, over his until he fell asleep. He told me he liked the weight of me and I'd smile at him, "I'm the blob," I'd say, "and you're Steve McQueen."

Sometimes, when he needed to escape from the prison of his bed, I'd pull him down to me on the floor, cradle the bones of him and touch him everywhere to keep myself from running away.

I bent down and kissed the sleeping baby on the back of the neck, it's soft, damp skin new to my lips. I pulled the blanket up over his arms and tucked it in tightly around his head. "I could come to love you, too." I said.

I fell asleep on the sofa and woke up slowly a few hours later. I'd accustomed myself to short stretches of sleep as my body would automatically tick away the hours between administering Paul's medicines. I looked at the clock over the television when I woke. 2:30 A.M.

I went to the window and stared out into the street. Christmas lights still flickered and burned along the eaves and in the windows of the houses and apartment buildings, their colors reflecting in the snow covering the front yards. I saw shapes moving across a window beyond the two sets of cars lining the street and a couple of doors down. Their tree was still lit. I watched them putting out gifts for their children around the living room, in separate chairs for each of the kids. I imagined them finishing, then going upstairs to make love because it was Christmas Eve and that is what they did every year since the mornings had gotten too hectic.

I turned to my own tree, carelessly thrown together, ornaments needing replacement, their brittle surfaces scratched and beaten by a succession of kittens and puppies Paul captured on the street. We'd nurture them until they turned into cats and dogs that we'd no longer be able to keep because of the clause in our lease. We'd smother them with love that would bridge our own between the slow periods of our entanglement.

I went to the baby's room. I watched him sleep. How does he sleep in such uncomfortable positions? And in a bed that crackles from a plastic covered mattress supported by moveable parts of iron and steel? Suddenly, I became afraid of crib death, chicken pox, the measles or the thousands of other infant diseases. I went over to him to make sure he was breathing. I brought my face down next to his to feel his soft breath. I fell to my knees then, my stomach buckling under, folding my body in half on the carpet. My eyes hurt, my hands numb. There was nothing I wouldn't do for him.

I sat at the edge of the bed and pounded the carpet, then placed my hands flat over the scratchy surface. My head dangled beneath my heaving shoulders. I stayed like that for a long time, then got up and went into the adjoining bathroom that linked both bedrooms. I stripped, kept the light off and turned the shower on and stepped into the steam.

I saw Paul coming into the shower towards me, him stepping through the spray when we were younger, our bodies firmer, taught around the lines where our separate parts joined. I took the soap from its dish and moved it over my body which felt as if it had been cut off like a severed limb, the phantom sensation of his body against mine, his hands moving downward, palpable and urgent. The heat growing more intense, hotter. Our sounds echoed off the scrubbed tile. When I came, I felt the water peppering my body, slicing through me like shrapnel as I recovered.

I collapsed on our bed that had become mine only in the final months. The sheets had tugged out from the corners and floated loose like waves over the wide expanse. I pulled them around me and rolled from side to side to tuck them through my legs and under my back. This is what it must feel like as I tried to feel the weight of death. Indeed, during the remaining time Paul and I had, I'd slipped into trances, held my breath for as long as possible, or lay absolutely still to see how it must feel to be beyond life.

Every time it felt unsatisfying, as if I was cheating the real thing and I'd ask Paul what he felt and he'd shake his head. "It's like a slippery slide, like when we were young, but there's no end."

"What about heat or cold?" I asked

"How am I supposed to know?" Paul looked at me, his gray face gleaming from a layer of sweat.

"I just figured you'd had a taste of it, some experience when you sleep."

"I don't. I just sleep so I won't feel sick anymore. I imagine that's the best part about dying."

"Tell me you love me. I need to hear at least that." This is how our conversations would always end the last couple of weeks, "Please, it's only three words." I'd say this as I cleaned away the dampness from his face.

"I love you," he'd say, curve a dry lip over the washcloth and reach for a finger to bring into his mouth. I loved him in these moments because he still made an attempt at being sexual.

I went into the kitchen to look for something to eat. I'd forgotten about it at the market the day before. Everything I bought was for the baby. My cupboards contained small bottles of mashed food and boxes of powdered formula, but nothing to eat. I opened the refrigerator and stood in the light. It was empty save for a few vials of morphine I'd held on to just in case it got really bad.

I settled on a bottle of tapioca pudding out of curiosity mostly. It was so disgusting to look at that I was surprised that it didn't taste bad at all. As I cleaned the jar out, the spoon rattled and rung out through the apartment. I kept the noise up because it reminded me of sleigh bells and when I was a boy watching my mother, all business, feed my sister and brother.

When you're young, what you experience is very specific. You taste the lemon, not the lemon tree, you hear the anger, not the words, you see a kiss, not the love. Though there aren't many good memories I have of my youth, which isn't to say there were many bad either, I do remember the way in which my mother's rigid schedule worked. Our entire days were set to a plan instigated by her to ease the burden of raising three children born within three years of each other. But after eighteen years of this, my brother told me how it fell apart when my sister and I went off to college and he was the only one left at home, as if she'd suddenly burned out, lost interest.

Paul's sickness was like my mother's schedule. I returned to the narrow vision of it, perhaps just to get through each day, or because I was watching my own expiration, my last gasp for life. So now all that's left are the specifics; the drugs, the vomit, the endless shit in his underwear, and the three bottles of morphine keeping cold in the refrigerator.

When I was a child we went to visit my Grandmother. From her backyard, late in the afternoon of our last day, I watched the clouds spiral up into the shape of an overturned volcano against the mountains.

My Grandmother came to tuck me in that night. "Where do clouds come from?" I asked. She folded down the large quilt just below my neck and brought her gray-hallooed head close to my face.

"Air and water and wind," she said, forming her lips in an oval shape and blowing against my forehead, "I have a book I can give you in the morning."

In the car on the way home I learned about cloud structures and formations. I learned their names; cumulus, cirrus, cumulonimbus and so on. I learned about transpiration, evaporation, how the air sucks water skyward. I learned about cycles. Because of that, I vowed to live where there were frequent storms in winter and summer so I could see the endless sets of clouds sweep up the valley. Afternoons in summer, while Paul slept, I'd walk up to the park above us and sit on its slope to watch the build-up of thunderheads. I would take pictures. Our drawers are full of cloud pictures.

One day, Paul stood in front of me holding a handful of them. "Why the hell do you have to take so many cloud pictures?"

"Because they're always changing."

He fanned through the stack, "They're nothing but clouds."

"Yes, but they're all different." What I wanted to say though, was that I thought they were heroic because they could destroy, crack like cannons, or soften a mood. Instead, feeling like I wanted to argue, I added, "All your photos are nothing but you and your goddamned family." But Paul had a way of avoiding confrontation, so he just shook his head and went back to rummaging through the drawer for more of his family.

Many years later I lived with my grandmother. In the late afternoon we'd sit and drink jug wine, follow the sun over the horizon and talk. One night she was feeling the loss of my grandfather and said, "It's good to have a partner."

"How so?" I asked.

"Look what we're doing now." She fussed a bit in her chair, a big Adirondack she'd come to love. "Are you too cold? I could get a blanket."

"No, no," It was nice to have someone care for me only.

"During the nights before your Grandfather died, he wasn't sleeping well then, he'd reach under the sheets and pat my thigh." She took a sip from her glass, looked clear across the valley to the foothills. I let time pass because I didn't know what to say, but somehow I knew to reach over and place my hand over hers.

It was growing light. The sky was painting itself steel gray. Snow was imminent. You could tell because absolutely everything becomes silent. Cars slide by without engines, dogs bark without throats and the train, which runs along a corridor two streets away, glides along the rails.

I moved through the apartment, checked on the baby. I had turned down the heat when I put the baby to bed so I was just beginning to feel the cold on my naked body. I liked it for a change, but now it was getting to me. I pulled on a pair of sweats.

I'd committed a crime, inflicted myself on others. When the full weight of that hit me, I went into the bathroom and took out a syringe from the back of the drawer. I ask that no one pity me. I certainly don't. My life simply has come to this. It is dark all the time now and watching Paul.... well it's a trip I don't want to take. My grandmother resides in a rest home now, to my family I don't exist. There is no one left to care for me.

I went into the kitchen with the syringe, picked out a vial of morphine from the fridge and carried them into Paul's room where the baby was. I drew the drug from the small bottle and filled the plastic cylinder. My mind began flashing to and fro, from this to that, the people I've loved, then finally to Paul.

The last thing he did for me was move his head slightly and whisper, "Follow me, David..." And as I bent down closer to him, his last words imploring, hushed and whistling, quietly up to me like wind through a cracked window, he said again, "follow me through."

I took the syringe, slapped the crook of my arm, watched a blood vessel rise, then plunged the needle in. Then the baby woke and began crying. Not a single drop of the amber liquid entered my arm.

This was the thing that saved me.

So why kidnap the baby? I don't really know. Maybe it was the emptiness, the hollow space of our home, the light that settles on nothing. Maybe it was that I wanted to do something horrible in the world, take a feeling back that was mine, which I'd lost. Perhaps. I could have given the baby to Paul's parents.

Instead, I bundled him up from head to toe in a bright blue jumpsuit I bought, one with attached feet and hood. I changed his diapers. It was easy because it was something I knew about. He smiled up at me and I talked to him incessantly, letting him know every move I was going to make. I tickled the baby, shook his legs up and down, made blubbering noises with my lips. I carried him from the bedroom to the living room and set him down in the middle of the floor among the toys he'd played with the night before.

I went to the drawer where we kept the instamatic. I checked for film. I got a new roll and plugged it into the back, snapped a few frames off. I set it up on the T.V. and worried it into position. The baby watched me throughout. When I went to pick him up, he smiled again. "Keep it up for just a sec," I said. I went to the camera, pressed the time delay button and turned the baby and me towards the camera. We both smiled grandly until the flash.

It started to snow. I drove two hours to a different town. I stood on the stairs of a Presbyterian church, all sturdy and forthright. It was still early, but I knew people would be coming in for Christmas service. I wore a hat, thick glasses and a neck warmer up to my chin to disguise myself. I had put the baby in a box among warm blankets with a note explaining where he came from. A pastor came to the door adjusting his frock. I held out the box, which he accepted, and ran away.

That night there was a story on the news about the baby's happy return; crying mothers and relatives, glowing lights, wrapped presents.

The day after, I joined the throng of people at the one-hour photo shop. I milled around the mall, then went back for the pictures. When I got home I emptied Paul's family from their frames and chose the best one for mine. For the first time in months my head was clear and precise.

Acknowledgements

"*The Narrows, Miles Deep*" began as a poem and grew into something much larger during an extraordinary two years. It could not have been written without the love and inspiration of Jayson W. so many years ago. This book is for him.

During the writing, I had help with the manuscript from David Grove, a friend left over from the John Rechy workshop in Los Angeles. My Grandmother, family and friends kept me attuned to what's important. I'd also like to thank Jody Eng.

"*My Kid in Footlights*" was asked for by my thesis instructor, Elizabeth Cox, at the Bennington College Writing Seminars. It is her wonderful compassion and toughness that I'll always remember. My other instructors, Lynn Freed, Doug Bauer and Jill McCorkle were extraordinary. I also want to thank the entire community of writers there for their warmth and friendship, particularly my fellow students and muses: Judy Rowley, Rebecca Evarts, Kim Ben Porat and Kristi Gedeon and Michael Schiavo.

"*The Road to Alaska*" benefited from an amazing line edit by Max Steele, a former editor of the Paris Review, who's No. 2 pencil worked like a magic wand.

Special thanks to Adine Maron for her friendship and type design for the cover.

Tom Schabarum holds an MFA from the Writing Seminars at Bennington College. He has published poetry and essays in various journals including OUT Magazine. He was recipient of the 2010 Creekwalker Poetry Prize. His Chapbook, *"Swimming With Michelangelo"* is available at tschabarum@wordpress.com

His first novel, *The Palisades*, was published in 2010.

He and his dog, Buster, live in Seattle, Washington.